Thatcher Payne-in-the-Neck

YEARLING BOOKS are designed especially to entertain and enlighten young people. Charles F. Reasoner, Professor Emeritus of Children's Literature and Reading, New York University, is consultant to this series.

For a complete listing of all Yearling titles, write to Dell Publishing Co., Inc., Promotion Department, P.O. Box 3000, Pine Brook, N.J. 07058.

Thatcher Payne-in-the-Neck

BETTY BATES

DRAWINGS BY LINDA STRAUSS EDWARDS

A YEARLING BOOK

Published by
Dell Publishing Co., Inc.
1 Dag Hammarskjold Plaza
New York, New York 10017

Yearling ® TM 913705, Dell Publishing Co., Inc.

ISBN: 0-440-48598-3

Reprinted by arrangement with Holiday House

Printed in the United States of America

January 1987

10 9 8 7 6 5 4 3 2 1

CW

For GRAHAM, *who brought joy and warmth into our lives.*

Contents

Thatcher Payne-in-the-Neck

1

The Idea

Even though Thatcher claims he got the idea first, I'm positive I did. But it was almost a tie. One minute the idea wasn't there, and the next minute it was splashed all over the place.

We were in our bathing suits, sunning ourselves on the beach at Trout Lake with Hugo, Thatcher's miniature schnauzer. Thatcher was fried on both sides. You'd think that at the very beginning of summer he'd have enough intelligence not to get completely sunburned. Except for his mess of freckles, his face was red like some lobster. Not that I'd ever seen any lobsters, especially freckled ones, but I'd seen pictures of them. Plain, unfreckled ones, I mean.

"Race you to the raft," said Thatcher.

3

Before you could spit, Thatcher, Hugo, and I were churning through the water, which felt fresh and cool washing over my face. Hugo didn't go far. He got sidetracked by a stick. Hugo is easily side-tracked, and quite frisky and hard to manage. If I had a criticism of Thatcher, it was that he'd been careless about bringing Hugo up. Still, dogs are dogs, and I managed to put up with him. Dogs aren't supposed to be at the Trout Lake beach, but the place wasn't officially open yet.

Naturally Thatcher made it out to the raft first. He's the best swimmer in our age group. He scrambled up ahead of me, with his red hair slicked onto his head as if it had been pasted there, and he helped me up. He didn't need to, of course, but I think he likes to try to demonstrate that boys are superior to girls, which is ridiculous. Or maybe he does that kind of thing because we get along like ham and eggs, even though we belong to opposite sexes. He takes care of me, and I take care of him.

Like right then, when I snuck a look at his red nose and said, "Hey, Rusthead, you ought to do something about that sunburn."

"What sunburn?"

"Thatcher, you are ridiculous and preposterous, and you look like a lobster."

"Cut out the big words, Knobnose. You're talking

like my mom." He giggled. I giggled. He splashed water on me. I splashed water on him.

When Thatcher and I feel especially close to each other, we call each other Rusthead and Knobnose. It happens only once in a great while, when the sun is shining and the water's clear and there's nobody else around and we want to show each other we're glad to be together again at Trout Lake.

Now we loafed on the edge of the raft with the water cutting off our legs. We bobbed up and down with the waves, taking in the cottages around the shore. At the north end of the lake, five or six miles up, we could make out the Dockside restaurant just this side of town, and farther on, the bandstand in the park.

I'm a very sentimental person. I always get this sort of melting, lighted-candle feeling right down to my toenails whenever I come back to the lake.

We sat there for a while sniffing it all in. Finally I said, "Race you back," and dived in from a sitting position, which is hard to do.

This time I nearly beat him.

Hugo, who was wet and slippery, jumped all over Thatcher. He rolled in the sand, scattering it onto our ankles. I sat down, flipped my ponytail over my shoulder, and put on a floppy straw hat that used to belong to my mom, plus an old plaid shirt of

Dad's. I wiped off my legs and spread my beach towel across them. There was enough left over for Thatcher. I like to think I'm a generous person, so I said, "Put this across your knees, huh, Thatcher?"

"Quit giving orders."

He'd get bossy with me that way because he's seven months and six days older than I am, and because we've known each other forever. His family has been coming to his grandparents' cottage at Trout Lake since ancient times, and my dad is activities director there. Dad teaches swimming and organizes games and stuff. Thatcher's the best swimmer in our class, which, this summer, would be ten- and eleven-year-olds, me being ten and Thatcher being nearly eleven. Thatcher's crazy about my dad, who's taught him almost everything he knows about sports. Dad practically brought him up, along with a lot of other Trout Lake kids. Dad was coming here in the summers to our two-room cabin even before he married my mom.

I always get a lump in my esophagus when I think about my mother, because I never really knew her. She died when I was six months old, and my dad was stuck with me. He teaches gym and coaches soccer and baseball at the high school in Evanston, just north of Chicago.

Dad has never had much time to cook, especially

during the baseball and soccer seasons and the summers. Also, he never bothers to hang up his pants or take the dishes out of the drainer or even straighten up his activities papers. So I was kind of embarrassed when people came to our place. Sometimes I wished I had a mother.

Thatcher's mother's parents have been leading citizens of the Trout Lake Assembly going back into the Stone Age, when it was started by members of their church. I guess his grandparents just about founded the place. Every summer Thatcher's mom brought him up from Hinsdale, another Chicago suburb miles from us. They always stayed with his grandparents. His dad used to fly himself up on the weekends, before his little plane went down, with him and my mom in it.

That's what Thatcher and I have in common. That accident.

The way Dad told me the story, it was just after the July Fourth weekend. Our cleaning lady, Bianca, who always checks our Evanston house while we're gone, had phoned to say our roof was leaking into the attic. Since Dad was swamped with organizing teams and stuff, Mom got a sitter for me and flew home with Mr. Payne, Thatcher's dad. That next Friday, after the roof was fixed, Mr. Payne took off into a storm with Mom along, and, well, I never did get the rest of the story straight. I guess it hurt Dad too much to explain.

Anyway, it was nail-biting time all around. Dad blamed Mr. Payne, because he didn't think he should have taken off into that storm. Mrs. Payne, who is shy and quiet and neat and pretty, with wavy hair and eyes the color of maple syrup, let her parents do most of the defending of Thatcher's dad, which they did.

Of course, there hasn't been much back-and-forth among the grownups in our families, and I guess this situation has always bothered Thatcher and me. I suppose we feel we can understand each other's feelings. Maybe that's why we've been so close over the years, and why it doesn't matter that we belong to opposite sexes.

So there we were, the only kids at Trout Lake, because most people don't show up till as late as the July Fourth weekend.

Thatcher yanked his mouth organ out of his running shoe and began playing "Row, Row, Row, Your Boat." He never plays anything else. He starts out softly and ends up very loud, like a symphony orchestra. It's neat.

When he finished, he wiped the mouth organ on his knee to get the spit off of it. "It's good to get some peace and quiet," he said. "I'm sick of living in a cottage with a mother and two grandparents who've got nothing to do but tell me which pants to wear."

He'd told me that same thing over and over. I nodded in what I hoped was an understanding way and repeated the same thing I'd told Thatcher a zillion times. "Grownups are a problem," I said. "I think my dad needs a keeper. You should have seen the mess when I got home yesterday. His wet bathing suit was dumped on the floor so it made a spot that will be there till the place falls down. He was frying hot dogs, and the grease spattered all over the stove and into the Green Giant peas. And we didn't have any buns or any mustard. Not even ketchup, for Pete's sake."

Thatcher stuck his mouth organ back into the running shoe and scratched a mosquito bite on his elbow. "You're going to have to take over, Kib. Tell Coach you'll do the cooking." All the kids except me call my dad Coach.

"But I can't get groceries because I can't drive. And Dad always loads up on canned chili, which I hate. Anyway, I don't know how to cook anything decent."

"Try using a cookbook. And get Coach to take you shopping. My mom takes me sometimes." There he was again, trying to order me around. "Anyway," he went on, "you're lucky to have a dad who's good at sports. You take my grandpa. He's really okay, but all he wants to do is break a hundred on the golf course. What I need is a dad."

"Well, what I need is a mom."

That's when we quit talking and stared at each other. Then we both shook our heads and said, "Nah, it would never work."

But there wouldn't be any harm in trying.

2

Do You Want a Dad, Thatcher?

It's kind of amazing we didn't get the idea before. I think it must have been floating around my mind for years. But even though the thought of having Mrs. Payne for a mother had never come right out and bit me on the nose, I'd always admired her. Of course, she'd never gone out of her way to be friendly. She always seemed to be following her parents around like a dog on a leash. Still, whenever I ran into her playing at the tennis courts, or at the Friday-night square dance, or after chapel on Sunday, she'd give me a flickery smile. I'd notice the way her wavy hair spilled onto her forehead, and the way her eyes were wide and kind of surprised-looking, and how her monogrammed cardigan sweaters always matched her dresses. If Thatcher was with her, she'd drop her hand onto his shoulder, and I'd see the sparkle of her nails. I thought it was beautiful that she touched him that way, but Thatcher hated it. I guess he preferred the way Dad would grin and give him a wink when he struck somebody out at baseball. Dad always wears his cap backward, so Thatcher does too.

Now Thatcher ran his fingers through his hair, which had long ago forgotten where its part was. He yanked on his sweatshirt, which was so baggy it made him look like some Arab sheikh. But at least he wouldn't be getting any more sunburn on that torso of his today. He clamped his baseball hat on backward, so the back of his neck was safe too. His nose, however, was already peeling like an orange. "We've got to figure out how to get them together, Kib. The right approach is everything." He screwed up his face into a squint. Thatcher always squints when he's concentrating, like a little old man. It's kind of nice.

"Do you really think we should do it, Thatcher? After all, they're mortal enemies."

"Mm. Well, have you noticed that on TV, people of opposite sexes who start out hating each other usually end up smooching all over the tube?"

"That's only on TV. You know the old saying, 'You can take a horse to water, but you can't make it smooch.'"

"Do you have to keep hitting me with your old sayings, Kib?"

"They're very significant, Thatcher."

"Oh, sure. Anyway, let's give this thing a try."

"Okay. I'm dying to. But your mom is so much richer than my dad."

"Kib, will you quit stewing about unimportant things and think of a way?"

I thought hard. Doing the job was going to be a whole lot rougher than talking about it. After considering the angles, I said, "The first step is for me to keep telling my dad how much I hate your mom and for you to go around telling your mom how you can't stand my dad. That lays the groundwork."

"Some groundwork!"

"Look, if they go on thinking we like each other's parents, that would drive them away from each other."

"They couldn't be any more driven away than they already are."

"But my idea works backward. It gets them thinking about each other, and figuring they have to defend each other to us. It's reverse psychology."

"Hm."

"The next step is for you to nearly drown during swimming class."

"Me? Nearly drown?"

"It's only pretend, Thatcher. See, it would cause a whole lot of commotion, and someone would charge over to your place and get your mom, so she could come and watch my dad giving you mouth-to-mouth resuscitation and decide he's a hero."

"What she'd do is blame him for letting me almost drown. She'd probably think he was trying to pay us back for, um, you know what."

"All right, Thatcher, if you don't want to go along with an insignificant thing like almost drowning yourself, why don't you think of a better idea?"

"Look, Kib, you're the brains of this outfit, and I'm the muscle."

"Sure, Thatcher."

I thought some more.

Thatcher wiped sand off his ankles. Hugo scratched himself, scattering more sand.

"Maybe," I said, "you could insist that my dad come to your birthday party on the Fourth."

Mr. and Mrs. Dudley, Thatcher's grandparents, always gave a big potluck beach bash for him on the Fourth, even though his birthday is on the third. "I'm a firecracker that exploded too soon," he'd say. Everybody in the Assembly was invited to go and eat and to watch the town's fireworks after it got dark. Dad never went, though. He said he probably wouldn't be welcomed by the Dudleys. I imagined he still had some leftover anger inside him, too.

"Come on, Kib," said Thatcher. "My grandparents aren't interested in having Coach come to that party."

"And he's not interested in going. But if I'm willing to try getting him there, you ought to be willing to try and soften them up."

"What do you want me to do, take out their bones? Besides, if Coach did come, my mom would stay out of his way."

She probably would.

Thatcher slapped a mosquito on his knee and wiped the blood with his sweatshirt. "It's got to be accidental on purpose. Like if all four of us should happen to meet at the Village Market. You and I could set a time."

"Nah. Dad won't do stuff like that on schedule. I'd never be able to get him there at the right minute."

"But he's always on time for his classes and games."

"That's different."

Thatcher screwed up his light-bulb nose and rested his chin on his hand. "Rats!"

I thought hard. "Maybe we could sort of steer them toward each other at the first band concert."

Every Wednesday evening during July and August there's a concert in the bandstand in town, and everybody from the Assembly turns up. Now Thatcher said, "My family never goes to those concerts."

Well, *almost* everybody turns up.

I sighed and thought some more. "How about if you made sure your mom lost her scarf at the opening square dance? Then she'd have to go to Dad's office and ask him to look for it in his lost-and-found box."

"My mom doesn't wear scarves."

"Well, her sweater, then. Don't be difficult, Thatcher."

"I'm not being difficult. Look, what am I supposed to do, grab her sweater off her shoulders and hide it?"

"How come you stamp on every idea I get?"

"I won't stamp on the next one, I promise."

"Well, um, you could tell your mom you want her to talk to Dad about your swimming."

He swiveled his eyes toward me. "Yeah? What about my swimming?"

"You could say you want private coaching so you can be in the Olympics some day."

"Hm. That's possible. But how come every idea you get means I've got to do all the work?"

"I could come and watch your lessons, and you could get your mom to watch too, and I could keep encouraging her by saying how important it is for you to have parental support, and then you and I could disappear after your lesson and leave them together."

"Do you think I'm going to make some kind of exhibition out of my swimming lessons, with two females watching every stroke I take?"

"Do you want a dad, Thatcher?"

He looked at the sky, concentrating on a small cloud above one of the cottages across the lake. "Tennis," he said.

"Huh?"

"Look, you know how my mom loves to play tennis. She's always banging the ball around with Mrs. Polk after she gets here. I mean, Mom can hardly wait to get out there on those courts."

I remembered how she always looked, playing with Mrs. Polk, usually in a white shorts outfit, and hardly even perspiring, for Pete's sake. "Yeah?" I said.

"Well, why don't we both pretend we need pointers on our tennis to get ready for this summer's tournament. You get your dad out to the courts, and I'll get my mom. She'll be crazy to find somebody to play with right off."

"That's a terrific thought, Thatcher. Dad always brings his racket, but with all he does, he never seems to make it over there. So let's do it. Let's do it right after dinner. Let's strike while the idea's hot."

"Meet you at the courts at seven." He took his watch out of his running shoe. "It's dinnertime. You'd better get out of the sun."

"Sure, Thatcher, sure."

Every once in a while, Thatcher does come up with a smart idea.

3

Game and Set

I trudged toward home, passing the boathouse, the chapel, the Assembly hall, the tennis courts, the baseball diamond, and a bunch of cottages. I always love the part of the road that winds through the woods, especially before most of the cottagers have come. It smells of pines, and it's dark and hushed, except for the sounds of birds and squirrels and chipmunks. And mosquitoes.

In front of the Croydons' cottage, I found a leaf for my collection, a really nice specimen from their pear tree. A couple of years ago, I was rummaging around in a footlocker in our attic at home when I happened to spot a homemade book with the word *Leaves* printed on the cover. The pages inside had pressed leaves glued onto them that were only slightly disintegrating, and they were labeled with some handwriting I didn't know. When I took the book down and asked Dad about it, he told me in a shaky voice that it had been my mom's when she was growing up. There were some blank pages in the book, so I went on with her collection. Somehow doing that made me feel closer to her.

Our station wagon, with a motor sitting in the back, was parked in front of our cabin, so I knew Dad was home. When he first bought that station wagon, he nicknamed it after Leon "Bull" Durham, the Cubs first-baseman. Dad had planned to drive the Bull into town and pick up a new motor for the Assembly lifeboat from Ernie, who runs the boat-yard.

Inside the cabin, I stopped to set the leaf down and feed my goldfish, Nip and Tuck. The radio was blaring out the news of some train derailment, and Dad's wide shoulders were jutting over the stove of our peanut shell of a kitchenette. He was wearing his baseball cap. Backward, of course. Those big feet of his were bare, and he had on his green T-shirt with the hem halfway ripped out. "Hi, Kibby," he said, tossing me a smile.

"Hi, Dad." My fish food was getting low. I'd need more soon. Nip and Tuck were at the surface of the water, gobbling up the stuff I'd shaken into the bowl.

They were waving their tails at me. At least I liked to think that's what they were doing.

I shut the can of fish food and went into my bedroom to change. "Say, Dad," I called out. "I was thinking."

"Anything unusual about that?"

"Nah. Only I wondered as I went past the tennis courts just now if you'd do me a favor."

"Sure, honey. Anything."

"Well, you know the tennis tournament. I'd like to beat Amy Alexander this year. After dinner, could you and I go play so you can give me some pointers?"

"You know I haven't gotten around to playing tennis for years. All I do is run the tournament."

"I know. But you're a natural athlete and all that. And I want to beat Amy so badly."

"Kib, it's not whether you win or lose but how you play the game."

"So I can play it a whole lot better if I get some coaching. My backhand was rotten last year."

"Well, I can try to help. I do remember a few things from college."

After dinner, he insisted that we do the dishes before taking off. "First things first," he always says. It was way after seven when he dug his tennis racket out of the back of the coat closet. "Dad, are you, um, planning to go like that?"

"Like what?"

"Nobody plays tennis in a baseball cap."

"I do."

"Well, haven't you got a decent T-shirt?"

"Kib, we're not playing at Wimbledon."

I gave up.

The courts were completely empty. Where were Thatcher and his mom?

"Now," said Dad. "Imagine a square, with your left foot at one corner and your right foot at the other. When you hit a forehand shot, you move your left foot to the upper right corner, like this." He demonstrated in that smooth way of his. "And for backhand, you move your right foot to the upper left corner, like this. Easy does it, see?"

"Mm." I kept looking down the road for the Paynes.

"Now, here's how you hold your racket for the backhand." Dad went on and on, all business. After a while he gave me his raised-eyebrows look. "Are you paying attention, Kibby? I thought you wanted to learn something."

"Oh, um, sure."

We began volleying back and forth. Dad was rusty at first, but he got better and better with practice. Finally I spotted Mrs. Payne's mocha-colored Cadillac coming toward us on the lake road.

She looked like peppermint-stick ice cream in a pink blouse and white cotton pants. She nodded to Dad and me, while Thatcher and I did everything but hug each other to show our friendship. "Dinner was late," he muttered. "Grandpa's golf game took forever."

Dad and I went on volleying, and Mrs. Payne explained to Thatcher the right way to serve in that soft, woolly voice of hers. As they practiced, Dad kept turning his head toward the other court when he thought I wasn't looking. In a couple of minutes, I planned to suggest to Thatcher that he and I play together, since now we both knew what to do.

It was then that I made the tricky shot that barely dribbled over the net. Dad ran for it, tripped, and toppled onto the court, skinning his left hand and ending up face down, like some centipede. I tore over to him. "Dad, are you okay?"

He got himself into a sitting position, carefully keeping his back to the other court. "I'm okay," he said. The left side of his nose was scraped and bleeding, and I didn't have a Kleenex.

Mrs. Payne was on her way over. "Are you all right, Mr. Slocum?"

"I'm fine. Just fine." Blood was dripping down his upper lip.

She knelt on the far side of him. "What a shame!"

She reached into the pocket of her pants for a Kleenex and handed it to him.

"Thanks, Mrs. Payne." He wiped his nose and lip. He didn't even look at her.

"Can I help you up, Coach?" Thatcher was standing behind him looking uncomfortable.

"No, thanks," said Dad in a particularly loud voice. He got up very slowly, holding the Kleenex at his nose and shooting little sideways looks at Mrs. Payne, who was biting her lip.

I figured Dad was probably too embarrassed to get talked into playing tennis against her, but I had a different idea. "Dad, if you feel okay now, why don't we play some doubles? The kids against the grownups, huh?"

"Hey, let's," said Thatcher, forcing the enthusiasm into his voice.

"Maybe we shouldn't, Kib," said Mrs. Payne. "Your dad ought to take care of that nose."

That did it. "I'm fine," said Dad. "You start serving, Thatcher."

His nose had stopped bleeding, but it looked awfully red. Sort of like a rusty hinge.

When Thatcher served to him, he missed the ball by six inches. And he kept missing. Gradually Mrs. Payne took over, getting her racket on way over half the shots we made to her and Dad. Dad looked more and more foolish. Besides, he was getting a shadow on the left side of his nose. Finally it dawned on me that he had a black eye.

He must be just plain punchy. Probably he could hardly see.

Mrs. Payne had the sense not to say anything. She just kept on covering both courts without making it look too obvious. Once in a while Dad made a feeble attempt at hitting the ball, and a couple of times he even got it over the net, but we all knew who it was that was piling up their score.

When it got to be five games to two in their favor and we were changing courts, I said, "Dad, your eye's turning black."

"We really ought to quit right now," said Mrs. Payne.

"I'm not quitting," said Dad, clenching his teeth.

She shrugged.

It was her turn to make the serves, and she put so much speed on them that she aced Thatcher and me twice each. I mean, that ball zipped past me so fast I could barely see it. She did that on purpose, for sure, so she and Dad would win the set right off.

"Hey, that was fun," I said, trying to sound enthusiastic. "Let's play again sometime."

"Right," said Thatcher, putting on a fake grin so

you could practically see his tonsils.

Mrs. Payne stared at the net.

Dad just stood there with his racket drooped at his side. Half of him looked like an owl with a red nose.

He didn't protest much when Mrs. Payne insisted on driving us home. But inside the cabin he said, "Kib, how could you get me into a situation like that?"

"Look Dad, I didn't ask you to trip and fall."

"I don't mean that. I mean getting me into a tennis game with that Mrs. Payne."

"She's awfully good."

He stepped into the bathroom, and I saw him checking himself out in the mirror. Finally, after I'd figured the sight of his face must have scared him into a coma, he actually spoke. "Yeah," he said, "she's not too bad."

At least he'd admitted that much.

4

Don't Go Away

That night, Dad ended up holding an ice pack to his face with his skinned left hand while he wrote to his parents in Florida with his right hand. The next morning, he dug up an old pair of dark glasses with a cracked lens and put them on. With his scabby nose, he looked even more like half an owl. Since he was driving to the Assembly boathouse with the motor, he took me along, and I walked to the place where Thatcher was already sprawled out, toasting himself. He raised his head about an inch and a half. "What do you think, Kib?"

"I think the whole thing was a disaster."

"Yeah." He dropped his head. "Let's cool it for a while. I think my mom suspects."

"Your mom can really play tennis."

"Your dad could have, too, if he hadn't messed himself up. Is he okay?"

"Outside of the fact that he looks like one of those new modern paintings, he seems okay, except I don't think his ego's in very good shape."

"Well, if his ego is hurt, that must mean he cares what my mom thinks of him, right?"

"Right. So I guess there's hope."

"Yup."

Late that afternoon, as I diddled along past the Croydons' driveway toward home, I noticed a car stopped down the road, facing me. It was a Cadillac the color of mocha ice cream. No question about it, that car was Thatcher's mother's car. So that had to be Thatcher's own, genuine mom next to it, staring at what looked like a flat tire, and she wasn't very far from our place.

In spite of what Thatcher had said about cooling it, I couldn't duck out on a new opportunity when it came along and stared me in the eye. With my clogs flapping, I tore along the road. Mrs. Payne had on slacks and a blue-and-yellow blouse that looked extremely Lord & Taylor. Her teeth were set edge to edge.

"Is there something I can do, Mrs. Payne?"

She looked a whole lot different from yesterday. She actually looked helpless. She blinked back a tear. "Thanks very much, Kib, but I don't think so. The Polks wrote and asked me to stop off at their cottage to make sure the man had come to fix the hole in their porch screen, and now this. I must have driven over a nail." She swallowed hard.

"It's okay, Mrs. Payne. My dad can change your tire."

"Oh, no! I mean I hate to bother him. He must be feeling terrible after last night."

"He's really fine, Mrs. Payne. I'll go get him. We'll be right back. Please don't go away. Please!"

There wasn't much chance of her leaving, but I ran toward our place and cut in front of the Bull and across the yard as if my entire future life depended on making it fast, which maybe it did.

Inside the cabin, I nearly tripped over the table with Nip and Tuck on it, spilling water on Dad's schedule sheets. He was pouring himself a glass of ginger ale, barefoot, with motor grease all over his sweatshirt, and wearing those cracked dark glasses. He still looked pretty awful, but what could I do? "Hey, Dad, you've got to help Mrs. Payne. She's in trouble. Her tire went flat down the road, and there's nobody else around."

He set his glass down, dug his hands into his

pockets, and gave me his stony stare. At least I think it was his stony stare. I could barely see it through the dark glasses. "Tell her she can use our phone to call Dinty's Garage," he said.

"Dad, that's mean. I think you should know that she's crying."

"Crying?" He raised his eyebrows.

He was weakening.

"Yes, crying. Actually, she's practically sobbing. It's a regular stream."

I hoped I'd be forgiven for stretching a tear into a stream.

Dad's a sucker for an unhappy woman. When *Casablanca* was on TV, he could hardly wait for the commercials to get over with so he could go on feeling sorry for Ingrid Bergman.

He shrugged, swung around, and slipped into his loafers. "Okay, spook, where is she?"

Whenever he's emotionally charged up, he calls me spook. I just about dragged him out of the door before he could change his mind.

Naturally Mrs. Payne's car was still in the same place. She had the trunk open and was tugging at the spare tire, but she quit when Dad leaned over to talk to her. "I see you've got a problem, Mrs. Payne."

"Well, yes. But are you all right, Mr. Slocum?"

From the formal way they'd been talking to each other lately, you'd have thought they were back in the last century. But the way they were looking at each other wasn't one bit formal. Maybe that was because they were sorry for each other since she was in trouble and his face was banged up. Or maybe it was because she looked extra pretty to him with her hair all tangled up, and he seemed especially appealing to her on account of having come to her rescue with a scab on his nose. Whatever it was, her eyes looked as if they were ready to dissolve, and Dad's Adam's apple was working up and down.

I wouldn't have been surprised if guitars had started to twang in the background, or bells had rung.

Without looking at me, Dad said, "The jack and tool kit, Kib. Would you get them?" He groped for his keys and handed them to me, and I took off toward the Bull.

When I came back, Dad was leaning on the top of Mrs. Payne's car, chatting, and she was nodding and smiling. "Thatcher has a good pitching arm," said Dad. "I'd like to see him really work at his baseball, and his swimming too. He must have got his athletic ability from you, Maud."

Maud?

She turned slightly pink. "You've been a big help

to Thatcher. He thinks the world of you, Peter."

Peter?

With all that talk suddenly bursting out of them, as if they'd been saving it up over the years, I figured the smartest thing I could do was to hand Dad the jack and tool kit and vanish. Kimberly Slocum knows when she's not wanted.

In my bedroom, I changed into my yellow T-shirt and brown shorts and looked in the wavy mirror of the dresser. I ought to do something about my hair. Half of it had come out of the rubber band I use around my ponytail. I finally worked the rubber band out and combed the twists. I wished I had a French braid like Carey Sykes in my class at school, whose mom fixes hers fresh every morning.

I took my bathing suit out in back and hung it on the line in the clearing between the cabin and the woods, while a chipmunk checked me out from on top of a tree stump.

For our dinner, I sliced a tomato and set the fruit bowl on the rickety drop-leaf table. While I was opening a can of hash, I watched Nip and Tuck swimming around in their bowl and wondered how come they never got dizzy. Some people think goldfish are blah, but they're a calming influence on me. Tuck looked bigger than usual. That fish must be pregnant. I pictured swarms of wriggly baby fish

circling that bowl and felt a thrill at the back of my head.

By the time Dad came back inside the cabin, the hash was practically cinders in the frying pan. Not exactly a gourmet dish.

I wondered how well Mrs. Payne could cook.

5

Cram It, Thatcher

Dad seemed preoccupied as he came back in. Since his hands were grimy from changing the tire, he washed them at the sink before plopping into his chair and digging into the black hash.

"Did you get the tire changed all right?"

"Mmm? Oh, yeah, yeah."

"Did you hear bells or guitars or anything?"

"Huh?"

"Never mind."

He chewed slowly and swallowed. "You know, I think Thatcher might have a chance for the Olympics."

"You're kidding."

"I'm going to start coaching him in swimming tomorrow. Maud's going to do the timing."

"Maud" again. Timing. Swimming lessons. They must have read my mind.

Dad stirred his hash. "She's giving him private lessons for his birthday next week. Did you know he has a birthday next week?"

"Dad, you've known for years that Thatcher Payne's birthday party is always on July Fourth and that everyone's invited to the Dudleys' beach and that you've never gone because of the, um, problem, but that you always urge me to go because you don't want me to miss out, which is very generous of you."

"Well, this year I'm going," said Dad. "I want to see the fireworks."

"Sure, Dad." I wasn't about to let on that he was stealing the ideas I'd gone to the trouble to think up at the beach yesterday.

When I got back there the next morning, Thatcher was grinning in spite of his sunburn. "Kib, you're terrific. Last night Mom told me what happened, and this morning she forgot to put the salt in the scrambled eggs. If things start to heat up between her and Coach, my grandparents are going to start breaking glass."

"Mm-hm."

"How'd you work it out? Must have been really tough."

"It was tough, all right."

When I accomplish something, I like to get full credit.

"Of course," said Thatcher, "Grandma and Grandpa weren't around when Mom told me about Coach and the tire. They were out on the porch watching the sunset. But if our parents get really friendly, just wait till they find out. Hooeee!"

"Do you think it would be that bad?"

"You bet it would. After all, your dad hasn't been all that polite to them the last few years."

"Now, wait a minute, Thatcher Payne. It's your grandparents who weren't very nice to him."

"What are you talking about? They could easily have had your dad fired."

"Cram it, Thatcher. The whole thing was obviously your dad's fault to begin with."

"It was not. Anyway, your mom didn't have to fly with him. He was doing her a favor."

"Some favor!"

Thatcher squinted at me. I was about to decide that his squint wasn't all that endearing anymore when my dad putt-putted past in the Bull, tooted the horn, and turned into the road to town.

"Race you to the raft, Thatcher," I said.

Naturally he beat me, but I didn't especially care,

because winning put him in a good mood again. He even told me I had great form.

He and I had always avoided talking about the accident. Maybe that's why we got along so well, and why our argument had upset me. Maybe it was only that he'd had too much sun, but I made up my mind to be careful in the future. I had an idea Thatcher would, too.

When he played "Row, Row, Row Your Boat" on his mouth organ, it sounded a little flat, but I kept my mouth shut, and we were kidding each other in the old way before I left to go home for lunch.

Whenever I walked into our cabin, there was a musty smell that hit me in the face. I suppose it hung around because the place is so ancient that some of the floorboards are starting to rot around the edges. I didn't care, though. It was a nice, cozy smell. Now, when I got inside, the smell was tangled up with the smell of the groceries Dad had bought in town. "Did you get the fish food?" I asked him.

"Oops! I forgot. I'll get it next time."

I supposed I could manage till then. Still, I had to remember Tuck's condition. Maybe I should start giving her more to eat. Funny. Dad had never forgotten my fish food before. If he was falling in love with Mrs. Payne, did that mean he'd go right on forgetting it?

6

Fireworks

Over the next few days, Dad's face began to get back to normal. I'd nearly forgotten that he's not bad looking without a purple nose. He was giving Thatcher his private lessons, with Mrs. Payne doing the timing in a pale-green tank suit. The lessons always went into overtime, and Dad always had lots to talk over with Thatcher's mom afterward.

Cars were pulling into carports all over the Assembly, and Dad began to organize teams and classes. On the day before the Fourth, I was lying on my back on the beach with my eyes closed when a voice said, "Hiya, Kib." A blob of something fell on my nose. I smacked it, thinking it was some kind of poisonous scorpion, and opened my eyes fast. There was the round, beaming face of my best friend, Heidi

Gunderson, who puts up with me at the lake and also back home. "Sorry, Kib. I got carried away, and it fell out."

The blob was bubble gum. I brushed it off into the sand. Heidi picked it up and stuck it back in her mouth.

I sat up. "Hey, Heidi, when did you get in?" I could hear the sand grating in her teeth.

"Around noon. My dad drives as if he's piloting the space shuttle."

"I know." I'd had experience with her dad's driving.

Heidi spread out her towel, dug her round bottom into it, and leaned toward me. "Okay, Kib, fill me in. What's been going on around here?"

"I think Tuck is pregnant."

"Don't be dumb. Goldfish never have babies."

"They do, too. Otherwise they'd be extinct. Anyway, Tuck's awfully fat."

"That's because you overfeed her. Or maybe *him*. Tell me what's really going on before I explode."

I told her about Dad and Mrs. Payne.

"You're kidding."

"I most certainly am not. Wait till tomorrow. You'll see for yourself."

Thatcher, who had been out on the raft, showed up dripping wet. "Happy birthday," said Heidi.

"Thanks. You coming to my party?"

"I wasn't asked."

"Everybody's asked. Seven o'clock. Potluck."

Heidi knew all this perfectly well, especially since her mother always brought the spinach salad with mushrooms and her dad always drank three or four whiskeys and ended up singing "They're Moving Father's Grave to Dig a Sewer."

Since Dad had always avoided Thatcher's parties, I'd tagged along with Heidi and her parents and her seven-year-old brother, Gardiner. I did this in spite of the fact that it wasn't all that easy to wedge myself into their Mercedes because the whole family's built along the lines of the U.S. Capitol building. This may be because Mr. Gunderson owns a nut company, so they eat lots of pecans and things. Not that Heidi's exactly fat. I like to think of her as solid.

But this year I was going with Dad.

"I'm going with Dad this year," I told Heidi.

"Hm," said Heidi. "Has he checked with Thatcher's grandparents?"

"My mom did," said Thatcher, "and Grandma blew up. I thought she'd break a blood vessel."

"Dad's going anyway," I said. "He says he can handle the situation. We're taking potato salad."

"I can hardly wait," said Heidi.

For hours before the party, I helped Dad peel

and cut up a zillion potatoes for the salad. Whew! Anybody who'd volunteer to bring potato salad has got to be in love.

We turned up on the beach across the road from Thatcher's at six fifty-nine. Mrs. Payne, in sailor-blue slacks and a white blouse with a frilly collar, was spreading stuff out on one of those portable tables, and Thatcher was digging a finger into the cheese dip. Mr. Dudley, looking like a bald rabbit, chewed a cracker, and Mrs. Dudley, with her blue hair, bobbed around like his mate. "Do we have plenty of crackers, Maud? Well, how do you do, Mr. Slocum?" Mrs. Dudley gave Dad a look that should have gone out the back of his head, took the potato salad bowl, and dropped it on the picnic table as if it were a time bomb. "Why, hello, Kimberly. Thatcher, Kimberly's here."

"Yup," said Mr. Dudley, "Kimberly's here."

"I can see that," said Thatcher.

"Don't be rude, Thatcher," said Mrs. Dudley. "Maud, would you run to the house and get another box of crackers, dear?"

"Right," said Mr. Dudley. "Let's have more crackers."

Mr. Dudley always sounds like some echo.

Mrs. Payne shot a smile to Dad, shrugged, and

headed for the house. "I'll help," said Dad, following her.

"Maud can manage by herself, Mr. Slocum," said Mrs. Dudley.

Dad turned and winked at her. "I'm not so sure. You know how heavy crackers are."

"Leave them alone," said Mr. Dudley. "They know what they're doing."

"Right," said Thatcher.

Mrs. Dudley shook her head, while my opinion of Mr. Dudley shot up about seventeen notches.

It was a long time before Dad and Mrs. Payne came back, but by the time they did, the Polks and the Croydons and the Alexanders and the Gundersons had arrived, and Mrs. Dudley asked Mrs. Payne to light the torches. Naturally Dad helped her do that too. "I learned how to light fires when I was a Boy Scout," he said.

Mrs. Dudley didn't even smile. And after that she quit suggesting jobs for Mrs. Payne.

When it was time for Thatcher's cake, Dad and Mrs. Payne disappeared into the house to get it without being asked. This time I thought they'd never come out. Thatcher and I kept nudging each other and trying not to look too excited when the Dudleys happened to be watching. Finally Dad and

Mrs. Payne came, with her carrying an enormous cake and him bringing the coffeepot and ice cream and nearly tripping on the front steps because he was beaming down at her.

"Did you notice them?" I asked Heidi.

"How could I miss?"

"Terrific," said Thatcher. "I think we've done it."

It certainly looked as if our parents were reaching the point where they could barely breathe without each other.

By the time we'd sung "Happy Birthday" to Thatcher, and Heidi's brother Gardiner had spilled ice cream on my jeans, and Heidi's dad had given us his rendition of "They're Moving Father's Grave to Dig a Sewer," it was dark enough for the fireworks.

I looked around for Dad. He and Mrs. Payne were sitting at the edge of the torchlight, talking and laughing as if they were making up for lost time. I spotted Mrs. Dudley's blue head turning toward them, and back again, all during the show.

The fireworks were just as much fun as always. There were fountains that dribbled past the stars, and some really complicated rockets that made Thatcher and Heidi and the rest of us kids ooh and ah. The final one seemed to burst over the whole sky with all different colors.

"Wow!" said Thatcher.

"Yeah!" I shivered.

As Dad and Mrs. Payne came over to join the rest of us, Mrs. Dudley marched up to them. "Maud, I think it's very rude of you to let Mr. Slocum take you away from your guests."

Dad gave her one of his mammoth smiles. "I thought it was you who was the hostess, Mrs. Dudley, and I have to tell you I haven't had such a good time in ages. Thanks for a great party." He reached out and pumped her hand.

Mrs. Dudley blinked and sputtered. Thatcher grinned at me. And I grinned back at him, wondering what would happen next.

7

Are You Surprised?

The Dudleys must have decided that resistance was useless, because after that things zipped along. All during July, Dad and Mrs. Payne kept the whole Assembly buzzing as they hooked elbows at the square dances, or shopped together at the Village Market, or banged away at tennis in the evenings. After those games, Dad would come home shaking his head. "That Maud," he'd say. "She's some tennis player."

When they took Thatcher and me to those band concerts at the park in town, just about everyone in the Assembly would be there listening to the marches and watching the drummer with the sugar-bowl ears do his stuff. He'd been bouncing those sticks off that bass drum ever since I could remember. Meanwhile, Heidi's brother, Gardiner, would tickle the backs of our necks with a blade of grass, the little kids would stomp around in time to the music, the Assembly boys would try to outdo the boys from town walking on their hands, and Mrs. Payne would sit there in a sort of glow, saying over and over, "I just can't believe what I've been missing."

But most of the time, she and Dad were doing things without me along. One good thing about their shopping together was that she always remembered my fish food. I could even understand why they were making a sort of orphan out of me. After all, they had to get to know each other really well, and there wasn't much time.

Still, I was a tiny bit jealous, seeing how Dad felt toward her. I actually got slightly nauseated sometimes. I was eating dinner alone a lot, and one evening I had to watch Judy Garland in *A Star Is Born* all by myself when it came back on TV, because Dad and Mrs. Payne were playing doubles with the Polks and stopping over at their place afterward.

When Dad and I had seen that movie on our set at home on a snowy night, I'd cried. He'd come over and patted my arm and said, "Good for you, Kibby. It's always the brave who cry." He'd disappeared into our kitchen and come back with a sort of gentle

smile and two mugs of hot chocolate, and as I drank mine down between sniffles, I felt warm and close to him.

Now, as the final credits flashed on the screen and I ripped a Kleenex out of the box to dab my eyes, I felt far away from him. And I didn't feel one bit brave. I was just plain lonesome.

I didn't feel any better the next morning at breakfast, when, straight out of the blue, Dad set down his coffee cup, shook his head, and said for about the billionth time, "That Maud. She's really something on the tennis court."

Even so, I kept telling myself that in spite of some inconveniences, this kind of thing was exactly what Thatcher and I wanted. After all, the romance seemed to be sliding along as smooth as grease, so how could I object?

Besides, there were nice changes in both Dad and Mrs. Payne. He got a kick out of making her giggle at silly things he pointed out, like the way the Bull always sputtered and growled when he started it, or the way the gulls strutted along the beach. They even invented names for them, like Elvis Presley and Queen Victoria. Mrs. Payne seemed even prettier now, sort of blooming, with an excited look. And Dad got lots more conscientious. Whenever he went out in the evenings, for instance, he always made sure to leave me a phone number and remind me to lock the door. He'd never bothered before, even though we had a key hidden on the ledge over one of the back windows. I thought the idea of locking up was nutty, but he insisted, and I went along.

Around the end of the first week in August, Dad looked in my general direction over his Grape-Nuts at breakfast, cleared his throat, and said, "By the way, spook, Maud and I want to take you and Thatcher out to dinner tonight. Can you come?"

"Well, I could cancel my invitation to the White House."

He gave me a weak smile.

"Any special reason?" I asked.

He inspected his cereal bowl. My dad, the Invincible, was blushing. "There, um, could be." He began scooping up Grape-Nuts like some steam shovel.

When Thatcher and I met at the beach that day, he looked at me sideways. "What do you think, Kib? This is it, huh?"

"Maybe. Seems awfully quick, though."

"Well, you could look at it from another angle. You could figure they've known each other practically since Trout Lake belonged to the Indians."

"That's true. Better late than not at all, huh?"

Since we were going to the Dockside restaurant, which was on the lake and was the poshest place around, I wore my bilious green dress with the bow at the neck. It was too short and babyish, but it was the only dress I owned. Mrs. Payne looked like lemon sherbet and smelled like lavender. Thatcher had on a tie with his white shirt and navy slacks. By this time his face was the same shade of red as his hair, and his nose had peeled so much it looked as if it had been caught in some kind of machinery.

At dinner we talked about Thatcher's backstroke and the fact that I had made the semifinals in the girls' tennis tournament by beating Heidi. Meanwhile, Mrs. Payne and Dad were giving each other little nods and smiles. I was noticing how brown and healthy Dad looked, like some TV sports announcer, and how deep and strong his voice was, and the fact that he'd even shaved his Adam's apple. He listened to Mrs. Payne as if every word she said was some precious jewel. Maybe that's why she seemed so much surer of herself, and why she smiled a lot, so you could see the one crooked tooth on the left side that the orthodontist must have missed. Her smiles weren't wispy anymore. They came right at you and washed over you like a warm shower.

While Thatcher and I were gulping down fudge sundaes and Mrs. Payne and Dad were sitting back drinking coffee, Dad cleared his throat again. The ends of his mouth twitched. "What do you think?" he asked. "Do you think we make a good family?"

I had a feeling he'd rehearsed those lines, maybe in front of our bathroom mirror.

Thatcher looked him in the eye. "You trying to tell us something, Coach?"

Mrs. Payne leaned over and put one hand on Thatcher's wrist and one on mine. Thatcher didn't even flinch. "Peter and I are getting married. Are you surprised?"

"Um, well, um, yes and no." Thatcher's voice cracked on the word *no*.

I licked chocolate off my chin. "See, we'd planned—I mean, I think it's terrific, and so does Thatcher, don't you, Thatcher?"

"Right. From now on the swimming lessons'll be free, huh?"

The joke wasn't that funny, but we all doubled up with laughter and relief.

8

Petunias and Geraniums

It turned out that those two were planning a chapel wedding for four o'clock on the next-to-last Saturday in August, which was only about two weeks off. Mr. and Mrs. Dudley must have decided they might as well go along with the idea, because they unbent enough to say they'd have the reception in Mr. Dudley's garden at the back of their cottage.

Only close friends and relatives were asked. My job was to get people to sign the guest book at the reception, and Thatcher's was to give Dr. Carlson, the retired minister who handles our summer services, an envelope with a check in it.

Since the chapel is tiny, we all stood around outside before the wedding. Mrs. Payne was wearing pale-blue chiffon, which made her look like someone out of those paintings I'd seen in books. All she needed was a pair of wings. She'd asked me to call her Maud, but I was having trouble getting into the swing of it.

Mr. Dudley, in a green-and-yellow sport coat, and Mrs. Dudley, in bluish-gray to go with her hair, were obviously making the best of what they thought was more like a funeral than a wedding. Mr. Dudley was laughing a lot, and Mrs. Dudley was switching her smiles on and off like a light bulb. Some of Mrs. Payne's—I mean Maud's—relatives had flown in, including her sister from Connecticut, who kept giving people a piano-keys grin and was going to be matron of honor.

The Dudleys spent their time talking with their relations, while Dad and I and Dr. Carlson, with his white hair, admired the stonework of the chapel.

I wondered if I'd ever be able to call Mr. and Mrs. Dudley Grandpa and Grandma.

Thatcher turned up in his navy slacks and a checked sport coat and tie, with his hair combed for once and his head down. "Hi, Kib," he said, kicking at the grass. "My feet hurt."

"You look okay. In fact, you look nice. Extremely nice."

He did, if you overlooked the patchy nose.

"Thanks," he said. "You look okay yourself. I'm sorry you lost the tennis tournament."

I had dropped the finals to Amy Alexander, who's way over eleven and is very close to nine feet tall and has stork legs. "Thanks. I'm glad your mom won the women's tournament." I kind of had to force myself to say that.

I wished I had a new dress for the wedding. Only Dad doesn't't ever think about things like that unless I call them to his attention. I hadn't wanted to mention the dress because I knew he was having trouble scraping up the money for the six-day honeymoon at Mackinack Island. While he and Mrs. Payne— Maud—were gone, I was staying with Heidi. Thatcher thought I should stay with him and the Dudleys, who have a whole bunch of bedrooms, but I had absolutely slammed my foot down. Rather than park myself with the Dudleys, I would even put up with Gardiner. Also, I was looking forward to the day when Dad and Mrs. Payne—Maud—came to pick up Thatcher and me and take us home. This was probably the first time in my life I'd be glad when school began.

Dad and, um, Maud were planning to sell both their houses and buy one with plenty of space, but meanwhile we'd be squashed into the cracker box near my school that belonged to Dad.

Dad had asked Ernie, from the boatyard, to be his best man. Ernie showed up at five to four with his hair matted to his head. He tugged at his ear, stood on his right foot and then on his left, and smelled of whiskey. He made Mr. Dudley look like a midget.

Mr. Dudley looked up at him. "Well, hi there, Ernie," he said. "Hi there." Mr. Dudley had a way of repeating things.

Mrs. Dudley took a step backward and said, "Good afternoon, Ernie," to the knot in his tie.

I cried during the ceremony. The sun shone through the window over the altar onto the top of Dr. Carlson's white head, and on Dad and Maud, making different-colored lights in their hair. Dr. Carlson boomed out like an organ, and Maud and Dad answered him in husky voices. After Dr. Carlson declared them husband and wife with no one putting them asunder, Dad reached down and swallowed Maud in his arms, and their lips sort of melted into each other's.

Finally Dr. Carlson coughed, Mrs. Dudley raised her eyebrows, there were faint chuckles, and Dad and Maud pulled apart. Dr. Carlson blessed them, and they turned to us. Dad kissed me. Maud kissed Thatcher. Maud kissed me. Dad hugged Thatcher.

Maud kissed her parents and her sister from Connecticut. Dad shook Ernie's hand. Ernie grinned at all of us out of his moon face. And I dried my eyes with my wrist.

Then Thatcher had to go and spoil it. He marched up to Dr. Carlson, tapped him on the arm, and held out the envelope with the check in it. Right in front of God and everybody.

There was more laughter, louder this time, while Dr. Carlson turned pink and patted Thatcher on the shoulder.

The Dudleys' yard was like something out of the Home section of the *Chicago Tribune*, with pots of petunias and geraniums and floaty dresses and the smell of bug spray all over the place. Mrs. Dudley began to sneeze, and Mr. Dudley explained in a loud voice that this time of year was bad for her because she was allergic to pollen. Later on I saw her desperately searching in her purse for one more Kleenex, and Ernie gallantly went over and offered her his handkerchief, which looked like a sail from one of his boats. Mrs. Dudley actually smiled at him before she blew her nose, and first thing I knew they were carrying on a very lively conversation, like a rabbit talking with a bear.

While I sat at my guest-book table, Thatcher slipped me a punch cup full of some liquid that

tasted like rotten eggs. I took one sip. Anyone but me would have barfed, but I only spat it out into Mr. Dudley's bushes. "What are you doing to me, Thatcher, huh?"

"It's champagne, for Pete's sake. Quit wasting it." He gave me that revolting squint of his.

He seemed extra obnoxious, probably because I was now practically his sister, and I was stuck with him. I mean, he seemed to think I was his private property.

"Thatcher," I said, "I am not your private property."

I poured the rest of the champagne into a pot of petunias, which would probably proceed to die an excruciating death.

"Quiet, please, everybody." Ernie was standing with Maud and Dad. He had one hand on the beverage table, probably for support, because he looked extremely nervous. "Here's to the groom," he boomed. "Let's hope he'll find happiness with his beautiful new bride."

It could have won the record for the shortest toast ever made. On the other hand, it wasn't bad. Dad beamed. Maud beamed. Ernie beamed. Thatcher beamed. I beamed. Mr. Dudley examined his roses. Mrs. Dudley looked at the sky.

Something streaked across the lawn and smack

into a leg of the beverage table, which buckled. Glasses and bottles slid off, spraying me with champagne and splashing various liquids onto Maud's dress, Dad's suit, Ernie's socks.

And onto Hugo, who now sat very still, with his tail drooping as if he'd been caught laughing in church.

Dad and Ernie and Mr. Dudley and two or three of the guests got tangled up trying to straighten the table and pick up bottles and broken glass, while Hugo slunk through the garden toward the woods.

"Thatcher," said Mrs. Dudley, "I asked you to shut Hugo in your room."

"I did. Only I had to go back for the check, and I guess I forgot."

"Forgetting's no excuse, Thatcher," said Maud, checking out the wet spots on her dress.

As I wrung out my skirt, which smelled like more rotten eggs, I wished I were old enough to wear heels so I could tramp all over Thatcher with them.

Maud threw me a look of sympathy, but before she could speak, Dad took her arm. "Must be time to leave," he said.

How could they go off and desert me in my condition?

9

Nip and Tuck

Whenever we leave Trout Lake in September, something flips in my gastric area. I turn and look back and reach out and touch the trees with my mind as we pull away along the Assembly road. I get this lonesome, panicky feeling, as if I'm disappearing onto a whole other planet and will never make it back.

Thatcher always used to go back for Columbus Day weekend with his grandparents, because the Dudley cottage is heated, but this year things would probably be different.

I rode with Maud and my goldfish, and Dad took Thatcher and Hugo. Before we met for lunch at Lake Macatawa, Hugo had upchucked in the back seat of the Bull, and my plastic bag with Nip and Tuck in it had sprung a leak in Maud's Cadillac. Luckily a gas station man had supplied me with another bag, but there was nothing to stop the smell of Hugo's upchuck in the Bull. At lunch, Thatcher politely suggested he and I trade places the rest of the way, but I politely declined. Hugo was his dog, not mine.

That afternoon, as we drove past the steel mills in Gary, Maud asked me about all kinds of stuff, like what I like to eat and what my favorite color is. I told her fried chicken and tiger yellow.

"Mm, nice," she said. "I'll bet yellow goes well with those stunning brown eyes of yours."

Stunning? I checked her face to see if she was kidding, but she looked flat-out serious. "Do you really think they're stunning?"

"I do. You have extra-nice eyes. Didn't Peter ever tell you?"

"Nope."

"Well, you know how men are." Her voice was fuzzy and soft, and we laughed together. "Your hair's nice, too. Nice and thick."

It was thick, all right. Still, I'd never thought of it as anything much. I mean, it wasn't a color that looked you straight in the eye, like brown or yellow. It was a sort of oatmealy shade. "Do you, um, think it would look okay in a French braid?" I asked.

"Well, I should think so. Let's try it. Shall I fix it for you?"

"If you wouldn't mind."

"And we'll have to get you a yellow dress. We'll go shopping on Saturday."

That sounded fine to me. I even told her about my mom's leaf book, which was now packed in my suitcase under my pajamas. At home I always kept it in my bottom bureau drawer under my Joan of Arc book and the surgical bandage I'd saved from the time I broke my ankle and might possibly need again someday.

Maud and Thatcher had never seen our little house. It's nothing, really. Just a square box, sitting in a scruffy yard the size of my big toe, that needed paint on the window frames. In front, a window on each side downstairs, and a window on each side upstairs. Inside, a living room to the right of the hall, and a closet and kitchen with no dishwasher to the left. Chunks of paint peeling off a couple of the walls. Upstairs, one big bedroom, a bathroom, a linen closet, my room, and the closet-sized room where Dad kept his exercise bike, which looked as if it had been on Noah's ark. Streaks on the wallpaper that Bianca, our cleaning lady, hadn't been able to get off. A crack in the bathroom window that Dad had taped "temporarily" when I was in kindergarten.

It wasn't exactly Buckingham Palace.

Thatcher stood in the upstairs hall with Hugo, taking it in through the pores. "Some dump, huh, Hugo?"

"Thatcher!" It was Maud, coming up the stairs with a barbed-wire look. "You will not be rude."

I knew our house wasn't much, but I'd never noticed there were all those marks and chips. They'd happened gradually over the years, and now I was seeing them the way you suddenly see yourself in a long mirror and realize your slacks are way too short. Even so, it was my house, and the minute Thatcher knocked it, I felt mad. I was glad Dad was still in the downstairs hall.

Maud took a deep breath and bit her lip. "Well, now," she said, speaking up so Dad could hear, "why don't we get our things in, and then I'll treat you all to dinner somewhere."

Dad called from the downstairs hall. "You don't need to do that, Maud."

"I know. But you took me on that marvelous honeymoon, sweetheart, and I want to do this one thing."

"Okay, honey. There's a nice place a couple of blocks over where you don't have to be dressed up."

I'd been afraid it would be a problem between them that Maud had more money than Dad, but

nothing seemed to be a problem between them.

Dad moved his exercise bike to the basement so Thatcher could have a room to sleep in, and they set up the folding cot for him. For his stereo, Dad brought up an end table from the living room, and Thatcher had to use his suitcase for a bureau. When we found a new house, he'd get his own furniture back, but for now he seemed forlorn in that room. I lost my sympathy for him, though, when I heard him make a crack to Hugo about having to make do on a desert island.

That was going too far.

10

It's Hugo

The next morning, Maud gave me a French braid. Her touch was soft and warm on my neck, and so quick that first thing I knew the braid was there. She inspected my face in the mirror. "It does things for your eyes, Kib. Makes them look bigger and deeper."

"Yeah. Hey, thanks, Maud. Thanks a lot."

She smiled her warm-shower smile that showed the bent tooth.

Before Dad took off for high school that day, he kissed Maud. "Take care of yourself, sweetness."

Sweetness. I looked at Thatcher, and he looked at me. He rolled his eyes. I shook my head. What had we got ourselves into?

Dad hadn't even bothered to say good-bye to me, the way he always used to.

After Maud left to look at houses, I said, "Thatcher, have you been getting that left-out feeling lately?"

"Sure, Kib, but you'll get over it. No point in being a baby."

He was putting on his tough act. There wasn't any sense in looking for sympathy from him. I'd call Heidi. But before I could get to the kitchen phone, Thatcher had taken it over to call his buddies in Hinsdale and say good-bye. While he talked to somebody named Mark, he poured himself a root beer. He stood with his elbows on the counter. He rubbed his nose. He scratched his ear. He pulled up a chair and sat down. He took a swig of root beer. Finally he ended up on the floor. By the time he got to a lying position, my patience was gone. "Give me a break, Thatcher. I've got to call Heidi."

He actually said good-bye to Mark and hung up. "Okay, here's the phone, but don't talk all day."

"You've been talking all day."

"It's only ten-twenty. I'll give you five minutes. I've got eight more people to call."

I ignored him and dialed Heidi's number. "Hey, Kib," she said, "I've been trying and trying to call you."

"Thatcher's got the idea he's Alexander Graham Bell."

"Yeah? I wondered about you and Thatcher living in the same house. I really wondered."

Why hadn't she told me? I changed the subject. "You going to meet me on the corner for school on Thursday?"

"Well, sure. Don't I always?"

"Your five minutes are up," said Thatcher. He was standing now, and he drained his glass of root beer.

"Heidi," I said, "I'm coming over to your place." I banged the phone down and stuck out my tongue at Thatcher, who burped.

In a way I felt sorry for him, starting junior high without knowing one person. But when Maud offered to stick around out there to help him through registration, he turned her down. "Coach can drop me off. I'll be okay." The tough act again.

Of course, neither of us knew how long we'd be in our schools. It depended on when Maud and Dad bought a new house, and where. When Thatcher and I had planned for our parents to get married, I hadn't considered I might have to leave the friends I'd known my whole life and move to a strange place. The idea gave me a flipped-out feeling in my stomach. But nobody seemed to care, including Thatcher,

, who was half responsible for the whole mess.

The first day of school wasn't too bad. Nearly everybody was back, and now that we fifth-graders were the top class, the others treated us like big shots. After school, Heidi and I stuck around on the playground catching up on our friends' news. Then we headed for my house to have a quiet talk about our day.

From halfway down the block, we could hear yelling and laughing coming out of the doors and windows of our house. Inside, there were sixth-grade boys swarming around like ants. They were lounging on the living-room sofa and floor, grinning at us. They were in the kitchen, where Maud, back from house hunting, was pouring soft drinks. You'd have thought she'd ordered a bunch of guys from Marshall Fields's in assorted sizes and was glad they'd been delivered. We could hear more of them upstairs, wrestling with Hugo. "Well," said Heidi, "you don't have to feel sorry for Thatcher. Looks as if the whole school's here."

Ron Colwell, who was draped on the sofa, had been in our grade school last year. Definitely pure concrete from the neck up. Public Enemy Numbers One through Ten. He and I had once had a punching match on the playground after he accidentally on purpose beaned me with a basketball. Now he leered at me. "You mean to tell me you're Payne's new sister?"

"Right. I see he's turned this place into a monkey house."

"Oh, sure. We're all chasing our tails."

Before I could think of a snappy answer that made some sense, a crash came from upstairs, along with Hugo's barking.

"What's happened?" called Maud from the kitchen, as if she were asking the time of day.

"It's okay," Thatcher yelled down.

The boys in the kitchen and living room tore upstairs. "Now's our chance," I told Heidi. "Let's get Kool-Aid, huh?"

Out in the kitchen, Maud was drinking a glass of iced tea. "Hi, you two. How was school?"

"Not bad," said Heidi.

"I'm glad. Say, Kib, I think I've found a house for us out in Northfield. It's got plenty of land around it, and a nice room for you with a view of the woods."

So soon? And out in Northfield? I'd have to leave my friends. I wasn't ready. How could Maud sit there calmly sipping iced tea? She knew I'd lived in this very house almost since I was born, and she was ready to tear me away from it and every bit of my former life. And all for a view of some dumb old woods.

Without even seeing that house, I despised it.

Ron Colwell's voice came from the upstairs hall. "Hey, Payne, look what happened to the goldfish."

The goldfish. I quit stirring Kool-Aid, made for the upstairs, followed by Heidi, and dashed past Ron. My bedside table had been tipped over. My lamp was on the floor, and so was my goldfish bowl, in a puddle. Nip and Tuck were on the floor too, completely limp. I picked them up, dumped them into the bowl, and took off for the bathroom, screaming, "Thatcher Payne, you've murdered my goldfish!"

There was silence. Then Thatcher's voice. "I didn't touch your stupid fish. I haven't even been in your room."

I ran water into the bowl. "Well, then Hugo did it. Anyway, they're dead. All of them, including their unborn children."

Hugo's dog tags jingled as he slunk downstairs.

Thatcher turned up at the bathroom door with his friends behind him, to see Nip and Tuck floating on top of the water, definitely and completely dead. "You don't have to go around frothing at the mouth, Kib. There aren't any unborn children. Besides, you

can get more goldfish. They all look alike."

Zap! I threw the water at him, goldfish and all.

He spit and wiped his eyes. Everyone else yelled at once. Heidi shoved Ron. Ron whacked Heidi. Hugo's yapping came from the kitchen. Maud showed up in the hall downstairs with her hands over her ears. The racket had finally got to her.

I held the bowl in the air over my head, thinking of crashing it on Thatcher's skull, but only thinking. "All right, everybody," he called out, "shut up!" Everyone shut up. "Listen, Kib, some of us were wrestling in the hall a while ago, and Hugo might have gotten excited and run into your room and hit the table, and we might not have noticed, and I'm sorry it happened."

It wouldn't have happened if he'd trained Hugo right, but still he had said he was sorry. I lowered the fish bowl.

Thatcher turned and walked away, stepping over the dead bodies. "Stupid goldfish," he muttered.

If Heidi hadn't held me back, I would have gone after him with that fish bowl after all.

Maud didn't say one cross word to Thatcher about my fish. All she did was to ask him politely to wipe up the water, which didn't seem like very much punishment, especially since the other boys worked with him, making loud, nasty cracks and using our towels and washcloths. Some help!

Maud put Hugo in the basement, where he proceeded to whine and scratch the door, adding his racket to the rest. It was more than a sane person could bear.

"Heidi," I said as we sat in my room trying to listen to music, "I don't think I can survive."

"You'll get used to it." She had to yell to make me hear. "I had to get used to Gardiner."

"But he's much younger than Thatcher."

"Age has nothing to do with it."

I moaned. But naturally I couldn't be heard over the din.

When Dad came home, he and Maud hugged and kissed. "Guess what, Peter," she said. "I found the perfect house."

Not one word about Nip and Tuck. Two deaths in the family. Probably a lot more. And nobody cared but me.

At dinner, Dad and Maud were so busy figuring where to put the furniture from both families that they barely heard me when I asked, "Do we have to go to Northfield?"

Dad looked over at me. "You'll like it, Kib. It'll be hard to make the change, but everything will be fine in the end."

It was easy for him to say that.

11

Thatcher Payne Is a Pain

It seemed as if everything had turned upside down. Dad and Maud, who used to be enemies, were now friends, and with Thatcher and me it was the opposite. Whenever Thatcher played his mouth organ, I got up and banged my bedroom door shut. I wished he'd take "Row, Row, Row Your Boat" and dump it into Lake Michigan at the deepest part.

How had I ever got myself into this mess that there didn't seem to be any way out of?

On the other hand, Dad had actually quit letting his clothes lie where they fell. And I couldn't stay angry with Maud. Every morning we'd chatter away while she did my hair, staying off the subject of Thatcher. It turned out that she's artistic and planned to pick out the wallpaper and drapes and stuff for the new house instead of hiring a decorator, and Dad was all for it. But at breakfast on Saturday morning, Thatcher and I were still only grunting at each other.

"Peter," asked Maud, "you will be out of your bathrobe in time for our appointment, won't you, dear?"

"Don't worry, honey. I'll make it."

I turned to Maud. "So we'll be going shopping this afternoon, huh?"

"Shopping? Oh, Kib, I forgot." She closed her eyes and shook her head. "This is terrible, really, because the real estate lady is showing us that house in Northfield and then taking us to lunch and then showing us some other places to compare it with, and I haven't got the vaguest idea how long that will take. You'll have to forgive me, Kib. I guess I got too excited about the house hunting."

"That's okay."

"No, it's not, but there's nothing we can do about it. We'll do the shopping soon, as soon as I get out from under this house mess. I promise."

She and Dad bought the house in Northfield. It had four bedrooms and four full baths and four crab apple trees, and we were going to move in the middle of October. Thatcher put on his tough act again, making believe he didn't care. He wouldn't even listen when I complained to him. And every time I mentioned to Heidi that I'd rather walk over nails than take off for Northfield, she burst into such a mess of tears that I was afraid she was having a nervous breakdown.

Maud had been clearing things out of the attic and closets for the Salvation Army. Now she began packing some of the personal stuff and getting Thatcher and me to do the same. While I was at school one day, our house got bought by a young couple with two daughters. I never even saw them.

Dad and Maud took us out to the new house, which was white brick and air-conditioned. Most of the time, Maud was out there working with the carpet man or the painter or the kitchen designer, leaving Bianca to take care of the cleaning on Wednesdays. Maud and Dad did drop in for meals, and Dad made a rule that we weren't supposed to feed Hugo at the table. But he hadn't called me spook for days. In fact, he hadn't called me much of anything. Whenever he had free time, he seemed happy to let Maud drag him out to show him the new bathroom tile or carpeting.

Maud kept bringing home samples of wallpaper, and she got Thatcher and me to pick out some for our bedrooms. Mine had yellow umbrellas floating around on it, and Thatcher's had red and blue space-ships, for heaven's sake.

Mrs. Dudley called and asked us all up to their cottage for Columbus Day weekend, probably only because she missed Maud and Thatcher. I was look-ing forward to going, even though I'd have to put up with the Dudleys. At least we'd all be together with nothing to do but family stuff.

One evening early in October, Maud said, "Kib, I've finally got Saturday morning free. Can you go shopping? We could have lunch out at Northbrook Court."

"Hey, neat. Sure I can go."

"Great, honey. I can't wait."

The next day after school, I knew something was wrong when she put her arm around me. "Kib, honey, we're not going to be able to go Saturday. The landscaper called and said he was coming to plant the new bushes. They've got to be put in now, before the ground gets hard, and I've got to be there." She bit her lip. "But we'll go soon, Kib, I promise."

That was the last Saturday before Columbus Day weekend.

Heidi had asked me to go to the movies with her that night. "Dad and I will pick you up at seven. Be on time, will you, Kib? This may be the very last time we ever go to the movies together in our lives."

There were tears in her eyes.

"I'll be on time," I said quickly, looking away.

"*Green Thunder* is out at the Old Orchard," she said, sniffing.

I'd heard that *Green Thunder* had special effects that made Fourth of July fireworks look like small sparks. I hoped it wasn't a sad movie. Heidi and I had enough sadness in our lives already.

Around five o'clock it began to rain. At six-thirty Dad and Maud took off for some faculty dinner party, so Thatcher and I made ourselves roast beef sandwiches, and he ate his like some cannibal. He kept slipping little bites of it to Hugo, which he knew Dad wouldn't have stood for.

His manners were getting more and more atrocious.

"What're you doing tonight?" he asked with his mouth full.

"Heidi and I are going to *Green Thunder*."

He snickered, nearly choking on his sandwich.

"What's so funny? It's a good movie."

"Sure it's good."

"So how come you snickered?"

"I didn't snicker."

"You did too. And I wish you'd choked."

"Listen, Kib, all I did was ask you an ordinary question, and you had to jump all over me."

When I asked him about his plans, he set his glass down, ran his tongue around his lips to get the milk off, and rolled his eyes. "We guys could end up doing anything."

He certainly was acting strange, with all that snickering and eye-rolling.

The movie started at seven-thirty, so Mr. Gunderson and Heidi came by around seven in Mr. Gunderson's Mercedes. Heidi had on her navy-blue tank top that showed off her tubby arms. I ducked out of the rain into the front seat next to Heidi and, remembering Mr. Gunderson's driving, snapped the seat belt extra carefully.

"Hi there, Kibsy," he said, stepping on the gas pedal so we took off like a cork out of a bottle.

"Oops, um, hello. Mr. Gunderson, how are you?" My conversation wasn't exactly stimulating, probably because I was gritting my teeth as we squealed around the corner with our windshield wipers pumping.

"I'm fine," said Mr. Gunderson. "Just fine. Say, Heidi, did you bring something to drape over your arms?"

"What's wrong with my arms?"

"Sweetie pie, you know how cold those air-

conditioned theaters are. You'll turn yourself into an ice cube. We're going home to get you a sweater."

"But we don't have time," she wailed.

"We have time." I didn't doubt that he could make it home and out to *Green Thunder* with minutes to spare. At the end of the block, he did a complete reverse, skidding around like some race-car driver, and took off back down the street, just missing a red convertible. The Mercedes screeched to a stop in front of Heidi's big stone house, while the seat belt dug a path across my stomach.

"Come on in with me, Kib," said Heidi. "Got something to show you."

"What have you got?"

"You'll see."

The first floor of the house was dark. The front hall was ink-black, so I could only feel the thick carpeting under my feet.

"*Surprise!*"

Spooky figures had jumped out at me from the living room. Somebody turned on a light. There were the girls from my class, screaming and yelling and laughing and jumping up and down. "Hey," I hollered. "Hey, what's going on?"

"It's for you," called Heidi above the din. "It's a going-away party. You were surprised, weren't you, huh?"

"Sure. Oh, sure."

I caught my breath. Wow! A surprise party. For me.

12

Cyclone City

The girls were all there, fourteen of them. Even Suzella Wimble, who plucks her eyebrows and wears black dangle earrings. To school.

"Were you really surprised?" "We thought you'd never get here." "Hey, did we fool you?"

"Yeah, you fooled me all right."

"Honestly?"

"Boy oh boy, are you girls good at keeping secrets!"

"All right, everybody." Mr. Gunderson, who had barreled through the door behind me, gave me a grin. "I promised you two girls I'd take you to a movie, so we're going to have a movie."

It turned out he'd borrowed our reel of home

movies from Dad, the ones he and Mom took when I was a baby. While we waited for Mr. Gunderson to set up the screen, Mrs. Gunderson waddled in with soft drinks and set out a whole bunch of food, like potato chips and nuts, on the coffee table and end tables. Lots of nuts, on account of Mr. Gunderson's owning the nut company. Naturally Gardiner, who has ESP about where the food is, came clomping down the stairs and began to stuff his flabby face.

There are a few feet at the beginning of the film where I'm a baby and my mom is holding me. The film's kind of grainy, but you can tell she was dark and full of sparkle. Everyone shut up when those pictures came on. Everyone except Gardiner, who hollered into the silence, "Is that her mom?"

While people were shushing him, I wiped my eyes with my T-shirt. Then the film broke, and somebody turned on the lights, and everybody joked around while I pretended my eyes itched. When Mr. Gunderson got the film started again, there were shots of me alone, crawling around, banging the tray of my high chair, trying to find my mouth with a spoon. We all laughed a lot.

When the lights came back on, Heidi said, "Gardiner, get out of here."

"Why should I?" he asked with his mouth full.

"Because it's my party, that's why. Now, take off."

Mr. Gunderson finished rerolling the film. "Time to leave, Gardiner."

"Heidi," said Mrs. Gunderson, smiling sweetly, "you could have said 'please.'"

Gardiner took off, along with Mr. and Mrs. Gunderson.

Heidi turned on some radio music, and we all started jabbering at once. We talked about our homeroom teacher, Mr. Otis, and his big ears, and about Miss Aaron, our gym teacher, and whether she was in love with Mr. Otis. Carey Sykes did her impression of our principal, who wears her glasses way down her nose and makes every sentence sound like a question. I giggled a lot, but inside I kept remembering this was the last time I'd be sitting in Heidi's living room with these particular friends, and my throat would get a peculiar, stopped-up feeling.

Around eight-thirty, the front doorbell rang, and Heidi answered. Three grubby-looking boys jumped inside, nearly knocking her over. "*Surprise! Surprise!*" They were yelling in falsetto voices, and swishing around pretending they were girls.

Naturally it was Thatcher and Ron, along with a skinny boy whose name I didn't know in a purple

T-shirt with DON'T HASSLE ME on the front.

Now I understood why Thatcher had acted so weird at dinner. He'd known about the party. But how had he found out?

Those three guys were making mud marks all over the Gundersons' hall carpet. They hadn't even bothered to wipe their feet.

Heidi slammed her hands onto her hips. "You and your muddy feet, you get out of here. I'm not going to let you ruin my party."

"Come on, Heidi," said Thatcher. "We're not going to ruin your party. We're going to put life into it."

"Who is it, Heidi?" It was that sugary voice of Mrs. Gunderson's, coming from upstairs.

"It's some boys, Mom. They're spoiling everything."

"Did I hear Thatcher talking?"

"Uh-huh."

"Well, if Thatcher's there, it's perfectly all right. He's always so polite up at the lake."

If she only knew.

Heidi groaned. "Oh, Mom!"

"Now, you let those boys in."

The trouble with Mrs. Gunderson is that she's always seeing the good side of people. She's too trusting. Anyway, I think Heidi really wanted to let the boys in and was only putting on an act. I mean, because it's always exciting to have your party crashed, especially since you can go around talking about it later.

"All right, you guys, you can stay. But you've got to tell us how you found out."

"Yeah," said Jennifer Sung, "who told you?"

"Nobody," said Ron.

"Somebody in this place must have squealed," said Carey, giving Suzella Wimble a look. Everybody always blamed things on Suzella.

"Nobody squealed," said Ron. "We heard something, that's all." Naturally he'd never tell us. He always tries to act mysterious and superior.

By this time the boys had tracked mud into the living room and were helping themselves to soft drinks and food. After that it didn't seem like our party anymore. Ron turned up the volume on the radio to screeching loud, so we all had to holler at each other. DON'T HASSLE ME opened a bottle of orange drink so it fizzed all over the sleeve of Jennifer Sung's blouse and onto the carpet.

Once, while Ron was demonstrating a football tackle to Suzella, he rammed his rear end into the corner of an end table, and I was glad to see his face twist into an awful wince. He'd knocked the table over, and an ashtray was lying on the floor in little

pieces. "Nice going," said Suzella, glaring at him as if he were some kind of flu virus.

Later on, when Heidi brought in a fresh bowl of nuts, Thatcher got the bright idea of dancing around the room balancing it on his head. Of course it fell off, and nuts rolled all over the floor and under the furniture. While we were trying to pick them up, lots of them got stepped on and ground into the carpet. The Gundersons would be finding nuts under the sofas and chairs for weeks.

When we finally left, the place looked like Cyclone City.

13

She's Not Smiling

The next morning, I was the first one down. I called Heidi from the kitchen phone. "Heidi, are your parents up?"

"Uh-huh."

"What did they say?"

"Mom didn't say much. You know her. But she's not smiling. And Dad's furious. That ashtray was a Limoges."

I'd never heard of Limoges, but if the ashtray had a French name, it must have been valuable.

"Also," said Heidi, "we're going to have to have the carpet cleaned."

I wasn't surprised. "Heidi, I could absolutely curl up and die. After all, Thatcher's my brother, sort of."

"It's got nothing to do with you, Kib. Mom's taking the blame because she got me to let the boys in. She's going to see about having the ashtray repaired, and if Dad ever sees Ron again, he'll boil him in oil."

"That blister! I hope he wounded himself for life on that table. And I can hardly wait to get hold of Thatcher. I'll tear him apart."

I was scraping the last of my cornflakes out of a bowl when Thatcher wandered in in his pajamas, followed by Hugo. "Hiya, Kib." He actually smiled at me. He *smiled*.

"Well," I said sweetly, "I hope you enjoyed the party."

"Great party." He opened the fridge door and took out orange juice. I hoped it would give him ptomaine poisoning.

"Thatcher, would it interest you to know that the Gundersons are going to need to have their carpet cleaned?"

While I smoldered, he poured juice into a glass and sat down, crossing his legs to one side and dumping his elbow on the table. "I imagine they do that every once in a while," he said.

That did it. I leaned forward and grabbed his juice glass and laid into him. "Now you listen to me,

Thatcher Payne. The reason they're having the carpet cleaned is on account of the nuts you scattered all over, and because of the orange drink your skinny friend spilled, and because of all that filthy mud you guys tracked in. And furthermore, the ashtray that Ron broke was a very valuable antique. Now, I hope you're proud of yourselves, because you completely wrecked Heidi's surprise party for me. Mr. Gunderson's furious, and Mrs. Gunderson isn't even smiling, and I wish our parents had never met."

I slammed the juice glass down so the juice splashed all over the table.

For once I'd made an impression on him. He was staring at me with those rusty eyebrows of his raised practically to his hairline.

"Kib," said a voice from the doorway, "we could hear you all the way upstairs." It was Maud, thank goodness. She was sure to back me up.

"Well, Thatcher and his friends spoiled the party."

She came in and sat down. "So maybe Thatcher should call and apologize."

"Call and apologize! Is that all? The least those boys can do is go and clean that carpet themselves, and replace the ashtray with the French name."

"I thought you said Ron broke that."

"Sure, but—"

"And Thatcher spilled some nuts? Is that all?"

So she was going to stick up for her darling Thatcher.

Thatcher went right along with her. "Look, Mom," he said, "Mrs. Gunderson asked us in. We were invited to that party."

Dad walked into the kitchen and sat down. "Thatcher, you overheard me the morning I asked Maud to drop that film off at the Gundersons' for the party, didn't you?"

"Well, yeah."

"And you passed the information on to your friends."

I might have known it was Thatcher who spilled the beans.

"Look, Coach, I only—"

"Thatcher, you weren't really asked to that party. You crashed."

"Oh, come on, Peter," said Maud. "Boys do that all the time."

"That doesn't excuse them for wrecking the house."

"I'd hardly say they wrecked the house. The Gundersons should expect to have their carpet cleaned after they give a party."

"For Pete's sake, Maud. Just because the Gundersons can afford to have their carpet cleaned every

five minutes doesn't excuse those boys' carelessness."

"Carelessness? Come on, Peter, you know very well that Kib exaggerates things."

"Kib knows damage when she sees it."

They were fighting.

While they argued, Thatcher and I bobbed our heads back and forth like tennis balls, not able to believe our ears. At last I'd got Dad's attention, but this was awful.

Finally Dad and Maud quit yelling and just looked at each other. Dad caught his breath. Maud lowered her eyes. Then Dad reached over and covered her hand with his. "Look, Maud, there's no point in arguing. How about if Thatcher went over to the Gundersons' and apologized in person?"

"But that's such a hard thing for a boy to do."

"That's the point."

"Peter, I really don't think—"

"It's okay, Mom," said Thatcher. "I'll do it."

He knew he was getting off easy. It wouldn't be hard for him. He'd probably be able to twist Mr. and Mrs. Gunderson around so in the end they'd be thanking him for crashing, even though I had most certainly not exaggerated about the destruction. Well, maybe the ashtray wasn't exactly an antique, but it was valuable, all right. So why did

Maud have to imply that I was some kind of criminal-
type squealer? Dad must have decided to go light
on Thatcher partly because he thought you should
treat Olympic material like royalty. But mostly on
account of Maud. He never considered me anymore.

So why had Thatcher and I had the dumb idea
that Dad and Maud should get married in the first
place?

Thatcher went and apologized to the Gundersons
that afternoon. From what Heidi told me the next
day, I knew I'd been right about his being able to
twist the Gundersons around. Mr. Gunderson had
ended up patting him on the back and saying he
was sure he'd be more careful next time, and Mrs.
Gunderson had sent him away with a handful of her
Nürnberger cookies with almonds and icing on top.

After that I didn't give Thatcher the satisfaction
of breathing one short syllable in his direction. And
now that Maud and Dad were on good terms again,
they were so busy chattering about the draperies
for our new den that they barely noticed our exis-
tence. Did I have to get into another fight to get
their attention?

Since we were leaving for Trout Lake after school
on Friday and then going right into the new house,

there were cartons all over the place, ready for the movers.

On Thursday evening, I rounded up a baseball and bat and stuck them in the back of the Bull, where Dad would see them when he fitted in our baggage. I figured we'd be able to have a couple of family games. In my room, I packed most of my gear for the cottage in my duffel bag, leaving out the plastic bag I was using for my hairbrush and toothbrush holder and toothpaste. The last thing I put in was the leaf book. I was planning to see if I could find all the same kinds of leaves that were already in there, only in their autumn colors. Then I'd make new pages and fasten them in between the old ones and press the whole thing underneath the Chicago phone directory. It would make the book a sort of joint effort, and I thought my mom would have appreciated my working with her.

After school the next day, I dug my notebook and pencil case out of my desk. I said good-bye to Mr. Otis, and Mrs. Cartozian, my last year's home-room teacher, and Miss Aaron, the gym teacher, plus Jennifer Sung and Carey Sykes and the others. I even said good-bye to Suzella Wimble. After all, she had made that nasty crack to Ron at the party. Her earrings scratched when she hugged me.

I walked home with Heidi, the way I'd done thousands of times. When we got to my corner, we just stood and looked at each other. She sniffled. "You won't forget me, will you, Kib?"

I wouldn't act like a baby. I wouldn't.

"Don't be dumb, Heidi. I'll especially never forget the party you gave me. Honestly. I never will." Those would be my final words about that party, at least until I'm forty. "Anyway," I added, "I'll see you next summer."

"Sure, Kib."

"So I'm not even going to say good-bye. I'm just going to turn around and walk away, the way I always do when we come home."

I turned around and walked away. I walked slowly, and then faster, and then I began to run, with my breath coming in gasps. When I got to my house, I couldn't resist a glance toward the corner. She was still there, biting her lip, watching me. She gave me a wave like an empty sock. I waved back, and then I dashed into the house, holding back my tears.

14

Deserted

No matter how rotten I feel, I always get goose bumps when I'm heading for Trout Lake. This time the leaves were gorgeous on the way up, all yellow and orange and brown. Hugo sat between Thatcher and me in the back seat. For a while Maud got us playing three-thirds of a ghost, but Thatcher kept squinting that stupid squint of his and losing, and finally he said, "I hate this game. It's dumb," and refused to play anymore. What a balloon brain!

Maud frowned, but she didn't say anything.

Thatcher fished his mouth organ out of his jeans pocket and began to play "Row, Row, Row Your Boat." I forgot I had stopped speaking to him.

"Thatcher," I said, "quit playing that song. I'm sick of it."

"That song has been around for years, Kib, and you're the first person who's ever gotten sick of it."

"She's the second," said Maud. "Please quit, Thatcher. Enough is enough."

So Thatcher could get on her nerves too.

By the time we actually arrived, Hugo and I were both asleep. I woke up to darkness and the feel of a chilly breeze and the sound of Mrs. Dudley's voice saying, "You all must be starved. How do chicken and dumplings sound?"

"Chicken and dumplings," said Mr. Dudley's voice. "Now there's a meal for you. Help you with your bags?"

We finally got everything in. I had the extra room looking out toward the shadowy woods. The room had twin beds with two pillows on each one. A real waste. Dad and Maud shared her old room. Thatcher had his old room, too, and naturally Hugo slept in with him.

Since it was so late, we were all starving, and dinner wasn't bad. Mrs. Dudley served us corn on the cob and a neat salad with tomatoes and cucumbers and Swiss cheese with holes in it. Mr. Dudley looked down the table. "Say, it's awfully nice to have

all of you here. It's great to have our Maud part of
a real family again."

"Mmm," said Mrs. Dudley, giving Maud a worried frown.

That night I was too tired to unpack. I just got
the plastic bag out of my duffel bag and let the rest
go.

The next morning, Maud was down early helping
Mrs. Dudley get breakfast. When I showed up with
my hair dribbling down my neck, Maud gave me a
nothing look, as if I were yesterday's newspaper. I
guess she'd forgotten about doing my braid. Later
on, as we all sat on the back porch having breakfast,
Hugo raced out past the flowerpots chasing a squir-
rel toward the woods behind Mr. Dudley's garden.
When he made a fast dash back to the porch door,
the smell nearly knocked us backward.

"'Fraid he's met a skunk," said Mr. Dudley.
"They're over behind the garden."

"Thatcher," said Dad, "you rub tomato juice into
Hugo to get rid of the smell. I'll take care of the
skunks."

While Thatcher was hunting up some tomato juice,
Dad took the hose, found the hole where the skunks
lived, and shot water into it. "They'll have to move
away," he told Mr. Dudley.

"Move away, huh?" said Mr. Dudley, scratching

his bald head. "Never heard of such a thing."

Dad arranged the hose in a figure eight. I'd never seen him wind one so neatly before.

"Why, thank you, Peter," said Mrs. Dudley, who was wiping crumbs off the breakfast table. "You're such a help."

"Say, Peter," said Mr. Dudley, "how about a game of golf? You could borrow some clubs over at the course."

So now the Dudleys were getting chummy with Dad all of a sudden. Well, he'd seen the baseball and bat in the Bull. He'd even told me what a great idea it was to bring them. Naturally he'd want to have a game.

"The golf sounds fine," he said.

He didn't want to be with us after all. He was ready to desert us. He probably wanted to show Mr. Dudley he could play like Jack Nicklaus, and he hadn't even asked me if I wanted to caddy. "If you don't mind," he told Mr. Dudley, "I'd like to invite Ernie along."

"Ernie?"

"My best man, from the boatyard."

"Oh, right." Mr. Dudley cleared his throat, glanced at Mrs. Dudley, and almost whispered, "I think that might be a good idea, Peter. I'd like to get to know him better."

Mrs. Dudley's eyes had glazed over, but suddenly they brightened. "You know, I'd nearly forgotten what a lovely conversation Ernie and I had at the wedding reception. He's very fond of cooking, you know. He told me his recipe for sweet-sour pork, and it's delicious. Why don't you two bring him back afterward for a ham sandwich?"

I couldn't believe my eardrums. There actually was a tiny drop of warm blood in her veins. "Maud and I can have a long talk while you're gone," she added.

Maud, who was in the kitchen, must have over-heard. "I think I'll join the golf game," she called out, "if you men would like a fourth."

So she was taking off, too.

Thatcher had poured tomato juice on Hugo and taken him up to his room, dripping juice on the porch and living-room rug, which Mrs. Dudley didn't seem to notice. She was giving me a thoughtful look. I knew what she was thinking. She was thinking that she was stuck with me. Well, I didn't like being stuck with her either.

I wondered how they'd all feel if I walked out and never came back.

I picked up *House & Garden* and sat and read an article on how to make jelly until Jack Nicklaus and his buddies left, yammering about the tricky dogleg

on the ninth hole. Then I went upstairs to unpack
my stuff in the guest room. As I hit the top step,
Hugo, with patches of dried tomato juice in his fur,
sprinted out of my door and down the hall into
Thatcher's door. When I got to the guest room, I
found out why.

The floor looked like chicken stew. Pieces of my
leaf book were scattered all around, with bits of
leaves sticking to them. There was powdery stuff
that must have been the remains of some of the
leaves. The letters my mom had printed on the cover
of the book were twisted into crazy shapes.

This was absolutely the final straw.

"Thatcher Payne, you come in here!"

"For Pete's sake, Kib, why all the hysteria?" He
wandered in, took a look, and gave a whistle.
"Hooeee!"

"Well, what are you going to do about it?"

"Me? Listen, how come you didn't keep your door
closed?"

When I raised my foot to kick him in the ankle,
Hugo growled at me. There's no way you can explain
to a dog that you're the one who's in the right.

"Thatcher Payne," I yelled, "you get out of here.
I cannot stand being persecuted this way. I am sick
and wounded, and I am probably bleeding inter-
nally."

After he and Hugo had gone, I threw myself face down onto my unmade bed and proceeded to make an enormous, gloppy puddle of tears.

When I came to, I blew my nose and tried to think what to do. I couldn't complain to Dad and Maud, not that it would have done me any good. Out the back window, I could see Mrs. Dudley picking mums while sneezing into a Kleenex. No use looking for sympathy from her. I was alone in the world. Nobody cared about my problems. Especially not Thatcher.

Even though I didn't have any place to go to, I was going to go. And I'd never come back from wherever I went to.

I slipped my change purse into my pocket. It had all the money I owned, which was six grimy dollar bills and some change. I snapped my toothbrush into its holder, grabbed my toothpaste and comb, and dumped everything into my plastic bag. I'd have to leave my duffel bag behind because Thatcher or Mrs. Dudley might see me. Anyway, I wanted to travel light.

I snuck along the hall past Thatcher's room, where he was lying on his bed reading *Teen Titans* with his running shoes all over the bedspread. That might be the last time I ever saw him. Well, who cared?

Down in the kitchen, a fly sat on the empty tomato

juice can. I stole a slice of ham and made myself a sandwich and dropped it into my bag on top of my toothbrush.

When I opened the front door, a breeze cut into me. I'd have to leave my jacket behind, though. Mrs. Dudley was coming in from the garden.

I closed the door silently behind me and took off.

Where was I going?

I found myself turning left toward the boathouse. Something was drawing me to the cabin where Dad and I had spent our summers. I could give it one last visit. I supposed the Assembly would provide a bigger one now, since there were four of us. Only without me there'd be only three.

But somehow that cabin seemed right for me just now. Luckily it was in the opposite direction from the golf club, and I could use the key we'd hidden over the back window if it was still in the same place. I could stay there overnight and figure out what I was going to do with the Rest of My Life. I might even think about calling my grandparents in Florida. Maybe they still cared about me. If I talked fast enough, they might even wire me money for a new jacket, plus enough to get down there. I certainly couldn't make it on my own with six dollar bills, especially grimy ones.

On the other hand, they might not care. Maybe

I could go live with Heidi. She could smuggle me into her attic and bring me food. Only, Gardiner might find out in a few days and spill everything to Mr. and Mrs. Gunderson, and while her dad was driving me out to our new house in Northfield, he'd get me killed in some accident too bloody to imagine.

There must be a better way. When I got to the cabin, I'd consider all the possibilities.

I marched along with a nippy breeze ruffling my hair into more of a mess than it already was. The road led between the lakeside cottages with their shades down, on one side, and the water lapping at the sand on the other. The grass had grown tall along the edge, and there was milkweed and goldenrod. The Alexanders' driveway had a car in it. So they'd come to see the leaves, too.

I passed the boathouse and chapel and Assembly hall and tennis courts, where weeds were growing now. Beyond the baseball diamond, the woods road was dark and slippery with wet leaves. To keep warm, I kept rubbing my arms. All around me was the smell of pines. The pears were gone from the Croydons' tree, and a couple of the lower branches looked bare and gnarled, which was the way I felt.

Around the cabin were little bunches of grass, turning brown. The front window seemed to stare at me. The front door, which Dad and I had hardly ever closed in the daytime, was closed tight. The top had been taken off the garbage can, probably by some raccoon, and lay on the ground upside down. In it was a puddle of dirty rain water.

Around in back, there were animal tracks in the mud. The key was in its hiding place, and I let myself in, glad to get out of the wind.

The musty smell was stronger than ever. The inside was just the way we'd left it last month, with rat poison in little brown boxes under the buffet and daybed.

I dropped my purse and plastic bag on Nip and Tuck's table, which reminded me of what Thatcher had let Hugo do to my fish without even caring. The sight of my sandwich reminded me of food, which reminded me of the going-away party Thatcher and his friends had ruined. Through the window the sunlight was spotting the leaves on the trees, which reminded me of what Thatcher had let Hugo do to my leaf book.

Everything reminded me of something horrible in my former life.

I flopped onto the daybed. For what seemed like hours, I lay trying to make myself figure out my future, but I couldn't concentrate. I mean, what can a ten-year-old girl with a toothbrush, toothpaste, and comb do on her own? I only got more and more disgusted and lonesome.

The cabin was quiet except for the sound of the wind making whistling noises in the cracks around the door and rattling the windows. I shivered. I wondered what the others were doing. Had anybody missed me?

It must be lunchtime. I got out my sandwich and ate it. It tasted like an eraser.

I lay down and fell asleep.

15

Remembering

"Kib! Hey, Kib!"

Somebody was rapping on the window. What window? Where was I? Wherever I was, it was getting dark.

Suddenly I remembered. I sat up on the daybed. There was a face pressed against the window that looked like a fried egg. Thatcher's face.

"Go away, Thatcher. Leave me alone."

"You let me in or I'll bust this window."

What was he planning to do to me? Well, I could take care of myself. I turned the latch on the front door and opened it. Hugo jumped up on me, nearly knocking me over, but Thatcher barely noticed. "What's going on, Kib? You lost your mind or something? We've been looking all over."

"Sure, Thatcher."

"Look, I'm not kidding. You got us all scared silly when you weren't around for lunch, and it was even a late lunch on account of the golf. Everybody's been looking in all directions, and I happened to think you might be here. We were all scared you might've drowned, for Pete's sake."

He always did like to exaggerate.

"I wish I had drowned. Nobody would have cared."

He stared. "You actually believe that?"

"Naturally I believe that. Maud doesn't care. Dad doesn't care. Your grandparents don't care. And you and Hugo both despise me. That makes it unanimous."

He'd been listening with his mouth open. Now he snapped it shut and rolled his eyes. "Boy, are you ever a prima donna! Do people have to drape themselves around your neck to show they care about you?"

"No. But I'd like a little civility once in a while."

"Civility, huh? You and your big words." He was holding my jacket. He'd remembered that. "Come on, Kib, let's get back before my grandma has a stroke. She thinks the whole thing is her fault because she was outside when you left."

So she was worried, too.

"Well, she'll have to go ahead and have her stroke. I'd like to know what she's ever done for me."

"She, um, well, she fed you dinner last night. Anyway, what have you ever done for her?"

That didn't seem like a very fair question.

"Thatcher, I'm not coming."

"Well, I'm not going without you."

"Just go back and tell them you didn't find me. You could bring up the fact that I might've gone to Florida."

"Florida?"

"Yeah. To live with my grandparents."

"Oh, sure. Do you think they'd keep you? Even if you could make it that far, they'd be sure to call your dad."

They probably would. "Maybe," I said. "But considering the way he's treated me lately, he wouldn't want me back."

"Kib, he's been all up and down the shore, running, calling out for you."

I pictured Dad, scared to death, with the corners of his mouth twitching, yelling "Spook" over and over. Pretty soon he might even talk Ernie into helping him drag the lake for my body. I shuddered.

"Kib," said Thatcher, "do I have to knock you out

and drag your body back to the cottage?" There was that word *body* again.

He was squinting at me, with ridges at the corners of his eyes. He looked desperate. "Come on, Kib." His voice was high and squeaky, as if it belonged to someone else.

"If I did come, you'd go right on letting Hugo get in my hair, and picking on me with your stupid pals, and wrecking my friends' parties. You've been just plain mean to me, making all those crude remarks, treating me like some bone that Hugo dragged in." My hands were fists now. "Bet you didn't even want your mom to marry my dad. Bet you wanted to keep her to yourself."

His face went red. "All right, look who's talking. You're the one who ran away because you weren't getting everybody's complete attention. Your dad spoiled you, that's what. I'll bet you didn't want him to get married either."

All I could do was sputter. Because in a way, I hadn't. Thatcher was right. We were both right. All of a sudden it was as plain as peanut butter that if you looked at the situation from a certain angle, neither of us had wanted our parents to get together.

We stood glaring at each other.

Finally Thatcher said, "You forgot to mention 'Row, Row, Row Your Boat.'"

I couldn't help smiling. I didn't want to fight with him anymore. I let my hands go limp.

He held out the jacket. "Let's get out of here. Let's quit wasting time."

I put the jacket on. "Okay. But I've got to lock the back door. Meet you in front."

I latched the front door, but somehow I couldn't leave quite yet. I poked my head into my little bedroom, where Dad used to read me to sleep when I was small. There was the chair where he'd sat, next to my cot, and there was my dresser, and the window where I could look out into the woods back of us to watch birds and chipmunks.

On my way through the living room, I picked up the plastic bag and checked out the crack in the window I'd once accidentally made with my tennis racket, the spot on the floor where Dad had dumped his wet bathing suit, and the marked-up table where we ate our meals. In spite of the rat poison, everything looked snug to me now. I stood in the middle of the floor, taking in the musty smell of the floorboards, and remembering.

It was true all right. I missed my life alone with Dad.

Very slowly I backed out of the cabin, closed and

locked the door, and walked around to the front, where Thatcher and Hugo were waiting in the dim light. Hugo's coat was still flecked with spots of dried tomato juice.

As we scuffed along, Thatcher reached down and picked up a stick. He kept turning it around in his hands. Finally I said, "I guess we're stuck with the setup we've got, Thatcher. Looks as if we're going to have to live with it."

"Right." He broke the stick and threw the pieces away. "Even regular sisters and brothers fight sometimes, and I can take it if you can."

I thought of Heidi's brother, Gardiner. Probably he was even harder to put up with than Thatcher.

We tramped on down the woods road with Hugo ahead of us making side trips among the shadows of the trees.

"Hey, Thatcher."

"Yeah?"

"Are you scared?"

"Scared? You mean am I scared of woods?"

"Uh-uh. I mean are you scared of going to a new school? I've never been to a new school."

He took a long time to answer. At last he said, "Yeah. I'm scared. Just a little."

"Were you scared when you started junior high?"

"Sort of. But you get over it, Kib. The feeling

goes away right off. Well, pretty soon, anyway."

"Maybe I won't be able to make any friends."

"Sure you will. You're okay."

"Thanks, Thatcher. I appreciate your saying that.
But I'll never have another friend like Heidi."

"You'll still be seeing her up here."

"So will you, and I don't see how you'll be able
to face her after the way you and your friends treated
her and her family."

"Oh, that. Well, see, I got the other two guys to
go around after school yesterday and tell Mrs. Gunderson they were sorry and ask what they could do
to make up for what we did."

"Thatcher, you don't actually believe Ron Colwell
would do that, do you?"

"Look, Colwell's not so bad. I'm positive he went."

"You're kidding."

"I never kid."

"Ha!"

He stooped and picked up a maple leaf. "This
okay for your leaf book?"

"My book's wrecked, remember?"

"You could start a new one."

The leaf was a perfect shape, and the color of
Thatcher's hair. "Well, maybe." I could do it in mem-
ory of my mom.

Thatcher found a good oak leaf, and a birch. I

spotted a pear leaf at the Croydon place, and farther on, a cottonwood. Thatcher handed me a cluster of pine needles. "That's no leaf, Thatcher."

"It is too. Pine needles are leaves. I learned that in science."

"Oh. Well, thanks a bunch."

"I'll help you find green leaves next summer."

I was beginning to feel that the leaf book was ours, and not just mine, and somehow that was okay with me.

At the lake, we zipped our jackets against the wind. The raft had been taken in for the winter, and there were only ridges of gray water stretching toward the cottages on the far side of the lake, stuck in among the circusy colors of the trees. We didn't speak. Probably Thatcher, like me, was remembering the summer we'd just been through and thinking about the one coming up.

He nudged me. "Nice, huh, Knobnose?"

I nudged him back. "Sure, Rusthead, it's nice all right."

On the way down the lake road, I even stopped to pick some goldenrod for Grandma Dudley.

16

Not to Mention the Goldfish

If I'd set out to create a sensation, I couldn't have done a more perfect job. We met Dad coming out of the Alexanders' cottage, where he must have been checking on whether they'd happened to see my corpse. He gave me a hug that nearly busted my ribs. "All right, spook, what do you mean by taking off?"

Spook, he'd said.

"I just wanted to be alone, that's all. I didn't think anybody'd notice."

For a long time he stood with his hands on my arms and the corners of his mouth twitching. He nodded. "Come to think of it, Maud and I have been pretty busy getting to know each other, and with the moving and all. Look, I know it's rough when you're on your own so much. Besides, there was that business at the party, and you've had to leave your friends, and I see Hugo got to your leaf book."

Not to mention the goldfish. Nobody ever remembered the goldfish.

"I'm sorry, Kibby." Dad put his arm around my shoulders as we walked along with Thatcher and Hugo.

At the cottage, Maud was on the kitchen phone in a powder-blue T-shirt and slacks, saying, ". . . may have taken the woods road. Are you sure she didn't pass your cottage?" Grandpa Dudley was coming in from searching the woods past the garden with burrs all over his slacks. And Grandma Dudley was plopped in the easy chair, fanning herself with a golf scorecard, in spite of the chilly weather. When she saw me, she hopped out of her seat, rushed over, and took me in her arms, crushing the goldenrod. "Oh, Kimberly, we were all so worried. And your poor, dear father was frantic."

She sneezed. I'd forgotten about the hay fever. Anyway, the flowers didn't matter. She'd actually missed me. When she let go, I went and dumped the smashed goldenrod in the kitchen wastebasket.

Maud, who had hung up the phone, hugged me hard. "Oh, Kib, thank heaven!" Her cheek felt soft against mine. "Honey, where were you?"

"At the cabin."

"So Thatcher was right. I thought he might be just now when I found the Polks hadn't seen you farther up the woods road. But why, Kib? How come?"

I shrugged. I couldn't talk.

She brushed strands of hair away from my neck. "We didn't take time for you, did we?"

I shook my head.

"You and I never even went to buy that dress. I'm sorry, Kib."

She pulled me to her, and I blubbered all over her powder-blue T-shirt.

For dinner, Grandpa Dudley dished up extra big cheeseburgers for me and Thatcher, and Grandma Dudley spooned mountains of mashed potatoes onto our plates. Even though Thatcher ate like somebody who'd just been rescued from a desert island, I tried not to let his disgusting manners spoil my natural good nature. I remembered to ask Grandma Dudley if her hay fever was better and to ask Grandpa Dudley about his golf game, and when Hugo licked my hand from under the table, I would have slipped him a hunk of hamburger if Dad hadn't been giving me the eye.

JudyBlume

knows about growing up.
She has a knack for going right to the heart
of even the most secret problems and feelings. You'll always find a friend in her books
—like these, from YEARLING:

____ ARE YOU THERE, GOD?
     IT'S ME, MARGARET $2.95   40419-3-39

____ BLUBBER $2.95   40707-9-89

____ FRECKLE JUICE $1.95   42813-0-52

____ IGGIE'S HOUSE $2.95   44062-9-80

____ IT'S NOT THE END OF THE WORLD $2.95   44158-7-36

____ THE ONE IN THE MIDDLE
     IS THE GREEN KANGAROO $2.25   46731-4-37

____ OTHERWISE KNOWN AS SHEILA
     THE GREAT $2.95   46701-2-17

____ THE PAIN AND THE GREAT ONE . . $3.95   46819-1-24

____ STARRING SALLY J. FREEDMAN . . $3.25   48253-4-15
     AS HERSELF

____ SUPERFUDGE $2.95   48433-2-83

____ TALES OF A FOURTH GRADE
     NOTHING $2.95   48474-X-83

____ THEN AGAIN, MAYBE I WON'T $2.95   48659-9-56

PEGGY PARISH

Perplexing mysteries for young people

Amateur sleuths Liza, Bill, and Jed spend each summer vacation with their grandparents on Pirate Island. And each summer brings a mystery more exciting than the last. Whether it's a frightening run-in with the eccentric Hermit Dan or an accident-ridden midnight foray into the woods, the dynamic trio is always stirring up plenty of excitement.

____ CLUES IN THE WOODS $2.75 (41461-X)
____ THE GHOSTS OF COUGAR ISLAND . . . $2.95 (42872-6)
____ HAUNTED HOUSE $2.50 (43459-9)
____ HERMIT DAN $2.50 (43501-3)
____ KEY TO THE TREASURE $2.95 (44438-1)
____ PIRATE ISLAND ADVENTURE $2.75 (47394-2)

YEARLING BOOKS